COLD CASE COMPLICITY
HELEN GRAY
Ozark Hills Homicide, Book 3

ISBN: 978-1-0882-5109-6

When justice is done, it brings joy to the righteous but terror to evildoers.

Proverbs 21:15

Chapter 1

Quincy Clark parked the Jeep she had been driving all day, pulling a covered tram loaded with tourists through the legendary Shepherd of the Hills Homestead. The warm, but not yet suffocating hot June weather was perfect for the Branson, Missouri, tourist season that was now in full swing.

Once she had signed off from her summer tour guide duties for the day, Quincy headed for the lot where her silver minivan was parked. As she approached the vehicle, she took her keys from her purse and pushed the button to unlock it.

When the doors clicked, she reached for the driver's door handle, but paused when a flash of movement drew her attention to the dark colored SUV parked the other side of her. Someone emerged from the vehicle and began walking around the back of Quincy's minivan.

At sight of the person a thread of unease shot through her. Then her heart rate accelerated. Dressed in loose khakis and a baggy shirt with sleeves rolled halfway to the elbows, the person wore dark glasses and had a beard and long, scruffy brown hair.

Suddenly the person rounded the van and ran up behind her, and the next thing she knew, arms swung upward and came down each side of her head, pulling a cord across her throat.

Acting on pure instinct, Quincy reached up and grabbed at the hand near her right ear. With stars and darkness flashing behind her eyes, she managed to grasp a pinkie finger and twist it backward. At the same time, she raised her foot and jammed a heel back into the attacker's shin, like she had been taught in the self-defense class her dad had insisted she take before enrolling in college.

There was a yelp as one end of the cord swung loose. Quincy whirled. With pain shooting through her head and throat, she swung her purse at the assailant's face, sending him stumbling backward.

"What's going on here?" a feminine voice yelled, footsteps approaching at a run.

At the sound, the attacker wheeled awkwardly, struggled for footing, and ran back around her van to the other car. Within seconds the motor revved to life, and then the vehicle roared away.

Quincy sank to her knees, her hands over her throat. Dizzy and weak, she swayed and sank to a sitting position, her hands still covering her throbbing throat.

A woman ran up and squatted beside her. "Let me see." Her voice was gentle yet authoritative. "I'm a former EMT, and I've dialed the police."

Quincy didn't protest as the short redhead removed her hands from her throat and peered at the injury. "I think it's just a surface wound, but you should have medical attention. I'll call an ambulance."

Quincy raised a hand in protest. "No. I don't want that. I'll be fine." She coughed.

The woman studied her in the waning sunlight. "Is there anyone I can call?"

"I'm new in town. Don't know anyone," she forced past constricted throat muscles.

At that moment a uniformed security guard arrived on foot and crouched beside her. At the same time, a police cruiser careened into the lot.

"Will you let me take you to my hotel room after you speak to the police?" the woman who claimed to be a former EMT asked.

"I know her," the security guard said, reading the uncertainty Quincy couldn't hide. "She's the director of a home health center in Springfield. Can you tell us what happened?"

By now a man wearing dark slacks and a lightweight blazer had emerged from the police cruiser and joined them. He sank down beside the guard and former EMT. "I'm Detective Booker, and I was only a block away. Can you tell me what happened?"

Quincy coughed again and gulped a deep breath. "As I started to get in my car, someone got out of a car that was parked over there," she pointed, "and came around behind me. Then he put a cord around my neck and tried to strangle me."

"Do you know who it was?"

She started to shake her head, but stopped at the head pounding the movement caused. "I have no idea." She coughed some more.

"Do you know why you were attacked?"

"No."

"If you won't go to the hospital, will you let me take you to my hotel room and treat you? I have a first aid kit in the trunk of my car—if they approve it," the redhead added, indicating the cops with a head motion. "They can follow us and ask their questions when I'm done with you. It's only a couple of miles. And I'll bring you back to get your car afterward."

"What's your name?" the officer asked Quincy.

"Quincy Clark," she whispered hoarsely.

He addressed the security guard. "You go on about your duties and report this incident to your boss. I'll follow them to the hotel. I know Miss Brewer personally and can assure Miss Clark she's in good hands."

The guard nodded agreement, but he helped the detective assist Quincy to her feet and escort her behind Miss Brewer to her car before leaving.

"I called my fiancé," the redhead said as Quincy was assisted into the passenger seat of her van. "He'll meet us at the hotel. He's a detective with the Springfield police department," she added before closing the door.

As the security guard headed back to his duties, the detective went to his cruiser. The redheaded former EMT started her car and drove off the lot. "I'm Ginger Brewer," she said as she pulled into traffic. Then she drove in silence, unbothered by Quincy's lack of response.

Minutes later, Quincy grimaced as her rescuer escorted her inside the hotel lobby and into an elevator. When they exited on the fourth floor, she kept an arm behind Quincy's waist for support and steered her to a room halfway down the hallway. Instead of using a key card, she knocked. "I have a roommate," she said briefly, shifting the first aid kit she had taken from her car trunk to her other hand.

The door opened to reveal a blond woman about Ginger's age. "Did you lose your …"

"No, I didn't lose my card," Ginger interrupted lightly. "I just had my hands too full to dig it from my purse. Erin, this is Quincy Clark. She was attacked in the Homestead parking lot and didn't want to go to the hospital."

"Of course." Erin stepped back, widening the door opening.

Ginger assisted Quincy to one of the two queen size beds in the room and proceeded to examine and cleanse her throat once she was seated.

"You're going to have some bruising, and it's going to

be sore where the skin is scraped. Do you have to work tomorrow?"

Quincy nodded. "I'm on the schedule. I'll be fine."

"You should apply ice to that throat every ten to twenty minutes and cleanse it a couple of times a day. You can take an over-the-counter pain medicine if you need it. I hope you'll take it easy for the next day or two. Avoid heavy lifting and drive as little as possible."

Quincy gave her a weak grin. "My job involves driving."

Ginger glanced over at her friend. "Erin and I are spending a few days here in Branson, taking some vacation time from our own work and planning our weddings. She's an optometrist, and I'm director of a home health agency, both located in Springfield. Our fiancés are sharing a room on another floor."

"I texted Miles while you were busy," Erin interjected, stepping over near them.

As she made the comment, a knock sounded at the door.

When Erin opened it, Quincy found herself staring at the detective who had been at the Homestead. Two handsome men accompanied him.

The detective spoke. "These guys were in the lobby. This one," he indicated the man on his left, "is DEA Agent Miles Jarrett. He's engaged to Erin. The other one is Officer Jon Zalinski. He's with the Springfield Police Department, and he's engaged to Ginger. They're both here on vacation, but they're obviously interested in this matter, since their women are involved."

Quincy blinked, trying to absorb all this as the trio entered the room.

Detective Booker approached, pulled a chair over near the bed, and sat facing her. "Can you answer a few more questions and repeat for us what you said back at the parking lot?"

She nodded, watching as the other two men positioned

chairs behind him. Speaking carefully, she focused on the detective and repeated what had happened. "If Ginger hadn't been nearby and intervened, I don't think I would have survived," she said when she finished, the retelling having brought a return of the shock and fear of the experience.

The officer's frown deepened. "You're sure you don't know who it was? Or why it happened?"

"I have no idea."

The DEA agent leaned forward. "Do you have any relatives or acquaintances with a grudge against you?"

Quincy gave him a weak eye roll. "There's very little family at home, and I hardly know anyone in this area."

"Where's home?"

"I live in Springfield, but I'm working at the Homestead this summer."

Curiosity sparked in the man's dark eyes. "Are the tourist attractions what made you choose this area for a summer job?"

She inhaled deeply, deciding she had to be honest. "No. I've been looking for my birth parents for years, and my latest information indicates they might be in this area."

"You're an adoptee?" Detective Booker asked.

She nodded briefly.

"Has your search yielded any names yet?"

She cleared her tender throat. "A DNA trail has led to possible relatives. The names of the people I'm trying to find right now are Drake and Janet Clayton."

At mention of the names, the detective's eyes reflected something she had trouble reading. Surprise? Interest? Knowledge?

"Do you know them?" she asked, unable to prevent the tremor in her voice as hope rose.

~

The Clayton names caught Delton so by surprise that his mind went into a spin. He had been working cold cases at his regular job in Springfield before being borrowed by the

Branson department for a few weeks during the peak of tourist season. They were already understaffed, and one of their detectives was out with a broken leg. Of the cold cases he had studied over the past months, the Clayton one had been of particular interest.

During his high school years in Springfield, he had worked summer jobs in Branson, an easy commute of forty-five miles. During those times he had become familiar with several families down here, and one of the best friends he had was now a member of the local police department.

His own first job in law enforcement had been here in Branson, right after finishing the police academy. A year later, he had quit to finish his college degree in criminal justice. Then he had gone to work for the Springfield department. The two bosses under whom he had served were friends, so when the Branson chief asked to borrow him for a few weeks, his Springfield chief had agreed. Now Delton commuted to work from his home in Springfield part of the time and stayed here with his buddy, Logan Fuller, when the schedule became too heavy. He would return to his own job full time when the injured man returned to duty.

Jon Zalinski was one of the Springfield officers with whom he normally worked, and they had discussed this particular case more than once.

More closely now, Delton studied the young woman whose feet dangled off the side of the bed. Wearing dark slacks, a tee shirt bearing the logo of the Homestead, and sturdy sneakers, she sat with her head down, long black hair concealing most of her face.

As if sensing his deepening interest, she raised her head. His gaze intensified, and she returned it through narrowed eyes, not smiling.

"How long have you been working at the Homestead?" he asked, recognizing that she was nervous and hoping to put her at ease.

"I only started the job a week and a half ago."

She was also sparing with information. "Who do you know who might have a grudge against you?"

She shrugged. "So far as I know, I have no enemies."

"Will you tell me more about your search for family?"

She nodded, clasping her quivering hands together and taking a deep breath. "I've known since I was eight that I'm adopted, but it wasn't until during a genealogy unit in a high school science class that I became curious about my origins. Because that made the project so personal, I continued the study on my own. The more I learned on the subject, the more curious I became. Through the rest of high school and college I continued my search and began digging deeper. I had no information about my birth parents, so I followed my dad's suggestion and began registering with adoption registries."

"Were you successful?" he asked when she paused.

She cleared her throat again, rubbing it gently. "No. But a couple of years ago my adoptive mother died from cancer. My dad is now confined to a wheelchair from crippling arthritis, and he's afraid I'll end up with no parents. So he encouraged me to have a DNA test done through Ancestry."

She paused again, her emotions obviously in overdrive at mention of her adoptive parents. Delton waited for her to regain her composure.

"That database came up with a match to a relative, believed to be the brother of my male parent," she continued, her voice growing a little stronger. "I searched for the uncle and found an obituary. The database also came up with a match to a cousin. With anything third cousin or closer, you can use the public trees of your matches, plus public records, to create your own tree and find how you fit into it. I haven't been able to locate the cousin, but the search eventually led to the names Drake and Janet Clayton. At Dad's urging, I decided to spend my summer break down here looking for them."

"It appears that someone doesn't want you doing that."

Enough so that they had attempted to end her search—permanently. "You mentioned a summer break. What kind of work do you do?"

She gave him a semblance of a smile. "I teach high school biology and chemistry."

He smiled. "Would I be correct in assuming that your search developed into a passion for science and your subsequent choice of teaching field?" He wondered if there had been more to it than what she was telling him. Did she feel abandoned and driven to find out why she had not been wanted? That was not uncommon with adoptees.

"You would." Her shoulders came erect. "Whoever just tried to stop my search doesn't know me. He doesn't realize that he's made me more determined than ever to find answers."

Something about her struck a chord with Delton. She was clearly intelligent and purpose driven. Delicate looking. But strong. And easy on the eyes. Her shiny black hair, heart shaped face, and wide green eyes were stunning.

Not things he should be noticing.

"What have you been doing to find your parents since you've been here?"

"I've visited the courthouse and the Recorder of Deeds office and chatted with some co-workers. I found no information about people by those names," she added, anticipating his question. "I plan to go to the library and look in their archives on my next day off."

"That sounds good, but I'm not sure you should spend time there alone right now."

Her posture became even more rigid. "I must be onto something. I can't let anyone scare me off so soon."

"I admire your gutsiness," he admitted, reading an edge of fear in her eyes. "And I understand your attitude. I'll accompany you. I want the same answers you do. When is your next non-working day?"

"Monday."

"Tell me where and when to meet you."

She smirked ever so slightly. "I'm staying in a camper at Table Rock State Park. Yes, I know it's an easy commute from Springfield, but I wanted to be here full-time so I can get acquainted with people and continue my search when I'm not working."

"That sounds like an interesting summer camp out." But not the safest, he couldn't help but think. "Okay, thanks for your time. Right now I'll take you back to your vehicle and follow you to your camper. Tomorrow morning I'll see if I can get a look at the Homestead's security footage of that parking lot. Then Monday morning we'll visit the newspaper office together."

What he didn't explain was that he would spend tonight keeping watch over her. It wouldn't be hard to blend in with the influx of campers and vehicles. He would also call his superior in Springfield and alert him to what he had learned that could possibly result in solving one of the cases the Branson and Springfield departments had worked on together.

~

The smell of fresh morning air greeted Quincy as she opened the door of the camper to peer outside the next morning. Sight of the tall, dark haired, out of uniform cop sitting in a dark, unmarked car across the road re-sparked the odd awareness she had experienced at meeting him after the attack. The last thing she needed was to get hung up on a guy she'd only be around briefly before going their separate ways.

He was bound to be hungry, though, if he had spent the night guarding her. She headed toward him, thinking the least she could do was feed him.

The car window lowered as she approached. She leaned down to speak through the opening. "I appreciate you being here, but it wasn't necessary. I'm going to fry some bacon and make some pancakes before going to work. I'd be happy to share if you're interested."

He studied her for several moments, as though judging her sincerity, before smiling. "That sounds good. Thanks." The window went up, and the door opened.

"My accommodations are a bit tight," she said as they entered the camper that her dad had taken on numerous hunting trips over the years. Although tiny, it had a kitchen area, sleeping and bathroom facilities—all she needed for a summer in the Ozarks.

"Nice," he said softly, scanning the snug quarters.

She shrugged, going to the small stove. "It's inexpensive and adequate for my needs. I have coffee made. If you'll be seated, I'll have food on the table in a jiffy." She pointed at the dining booth that consisted of two benches positioned against two walls at the corner of the room and flanking a small drop leaf table.

She sensed him studying her as she placed a coffee mug in front of him and filled it.

"I've been reading back over the missing persons case of the couple you're seeking."

Quincy frowned. "Missing?"

He nodded. "The woman's sister reported the couple and their baby missing twenty-five years ago, after being unable to contact or locate them for several weeks. They have never been found."

The statement brought a myriad of questions to Quincy's mind—and a niggle of unease to her spine.

"Your appearance and search for them after all these years," he continued, "has apparently stirred a hornet's nest."

Chapter 2

Delton watched Quincy square her shoulders, her expression morphing into one of resolution.

"That means I'm onto something, and it doesn't sound good," she said after several moments. "Which means the truth needs to be found. And that attack makes me mad enough to not let them scare me off their trail." She returned to her food preparation.

He had to give her credit for sheer courage, but it also gave him an increased dose of concern for her safety. She soon had food on the table and was seated in the bench facing him. He waited while she bowed her head in a silent blessing over the meal. He wasn't accustomed to the action, but it didn't bother him. In fact, he liked what it said about her character. Respect for her blossomed inside him—along with the strange awareness that he found unnerving.

"Where did you live growing up?" he asked once they had eaten, curious about her.

"Springfield, near where I currently live. I don't live with Dad, but I spend a lot of time with him since he's been so crippled with arthritis."

"Were your adoptive parents good ones?"

She smiled. "They were. I was very fortunate. They

were older, having given up on ever having children. They adopted me when I was almost two years old. I was eight when they explained to me how much they had wanted children, and how God led them to me. They loved me, probably too much," she added, her eyes rolling upward. "They spoiled me."

He tipped his head, sniffing. "You don't smell rotten to me. And you look great. Whatever your origins, you apparently had a good life."

Her expression went solemn. "I did, and I thank God for it. But I'm curious how it came to be that way. And why my natural parents didn't want me," she admitted, at least partially confirming his suspicions about her motive.

"I can understand that, as well as your dad's desire to know if you have more blood family that you should get to know. But you need to be careful. Apparently, someone out there doesn't want you to find out what happened to the Clayton couple."

She studied him through narrowed eyes. "You want to know because it's your job."

"Sure. But I'd also like to see you have the answers you need—and culprits brought to justice if they harmed those people."

She nodded, as if satisfied, and began clearing the table.

"I'll follow you to work and talk to the security guard. Then I need to get some sleep."

When they arrived at the Homestead, he watched her park her minivan and head to her Jeep. Then he went to the office, showed the woman on duty his credentials, and asked where to locate the security guard. She called the guy, and soon he and the guard were viewing footage of the parking lot from the evening before.

"There he is." The guard leaned forward and pointed at a figure emerging from the car next to Quincy's van. The attacker's face was not visible, as if the person knew where the camera was located and was keeping his face averted from it. And there wasn't enough of his car visible to identify the license plate.

Delton shook his head, hating the clearly planned execution of the attack.

After being assured by the guard that he would keep an eye on Quincy all day, he went to the police station and gave the chief an update.

~

Monday morning, Quincy pushed to her knees in the bed and peeked out the camper window. Sure enough, a police car was out there, with Delton behind the wheel.

She dressed quickly and went to the door. "Come on in and have breakfast," she called, beckoning.

He emerged from the car, wearing a somewhat sheepish look. "It isn't necessary for you to feed me, but I appreciate it," he said as he approached the camper.

She shrugged. "I have to eat. You have to eat. And it isn't any more trouble to fix for both of us instead of just me. How did your day go yesterday?" she asked over her shoulder, going to put on the coffee pot.

He took a seat at the table. "The security guard and I looked at surveillance footage, but we didn't see anything useful. Whoever attacked you must be connected to the Clayton case, because that's the only thing you've investigated in the brief time you've been working here. From there, I went to my friend's house and got some shut-eye before trying to locate the woman who reported her sister missing all those years ago."

Quincy whipped around, her interest instantly snagged. "You found her?"

"I'm afraid not. I didn't find anything indicating she's not still alive, but she's not living at the address in the files, and I couldn't find a new one. She could be living anywhere by now. I'll keep looking, though," he promised at her dejected expression.

"There had to be more family."

He nodded. "Let's see what we can dig up in the newspaper archives."

Quincy focused on the meal, but her mind spun in circles, wondering if she was wasting her time on this search, and whether it was worth the unexpected danger.

By the time they had eaten and cleared the table, she had concluded that, although the attack had fueled her curiosity as well as her anger, the end result was that her desire to find her parents—or what someone didn't want known happened to them—wouldn't be satisfied with anything less than the full truth. She wanted the closure of knowing whether they were dead or alive—and why they had not kept her with them.

"I think you should ride with me," Delton said when they were ready to leave.

Quincy didn't dispute his logic. It would be convenient as well as safer. And it felt good to finally have someone who also wanted answers helping in her search.

They arrived at the library in a reasonable time, considering the tourist traffic. When they entered the building and asked the librarian to direct them to the archives, they were shown to a small room where the walls were lined with shelves stacked with boxes of microfiche. A machine sat on a small table at one side of the room, two chairs near it.

As soon as the woman left, they began searching for anything they could find about Drake and Janet Clayton, concentrating on the time period shortly before and after Quincy's birth.

Quincy grew tired as she combed through countless newspapers and found no mention of a couple disappearing. "There has to be something," she muttered, leaning back and rubbing her eyes. "Two people couldn't just disappear into thin air. Here, you take a turn." She pushed the chair back and stood.

Delton sat studying the screen for several minutes

before raising a fist and pumping it. "Here's something interesting. Come take a look."

She took his place on the chair and peered at a black and white photograph of two couples standing next to a red Corvette parked in front of a theater. The guy on the right had dark hair reminiscent of pictures and movies Quincy had seen of Elvis Presley. His arm rested across the back of a petite blond. The couple to their right consisted of a guy with light brown hair, his hand draped over the shoulder of a woman near his own height. She had dark wavy hair pushed back over her ears.

Quincy stared at the theater in the background, a large US flag displayed on the doorway. She wondered if they worked there—and which couple might possibly be her parents.

"Country Cuzzins," she murmured, reading the name on the building. "I don't recall any theater by that name."

Delton leaned down to peer over her shoulder. "If I'm not mistaken, that building is now occupied by the Heartland Hoedown show."

Quincy took another look. The newspaper article below the picture related that the theater crew had done a special show on the Fourth of July of that year to benefit area veterans. The Clayton and Ramsey couples were reported to be ardent supporters of military veterans, each having family members who had served.

The thing that caused a ping in her mid-section was reading a notation that identified the couple on the left as Drake and Janet Clayton. She stared hard at the picture, searching for features similar to her own. Then she noted the date of the article. She would have been fourteen months old then, only a few months shy of the age at which she had been adopted by the Clarks.

"You look a bit like Mrs. Clayton," Delton commented, reading her mind.

She printed the article, anxious to have a true depiction

of the people who might have given birth to her.

"Make two copies of everything you print," Delton instructed.

She printed another copy.

They read a few more articles, but didn't find anything useful—until Quincy ran across an article printed months later about a Mrs. Jocelyn Rathburn reporting her sister missing.

Quincy set the print count to two, hit Print, and turned to face Delton. "I have to find this woman and talk to her. If she's still alive," she added, hoping desperately that was the case.

"I can help with that now that we have a name." Delton pulled out his phone.

Quincy gathered her purse, went to the front desk, and paid for the copies while he made a call and walked over to a spot near the main exit that was unoccupied at the moment. He dialed, and then spoke for a couple of minutes before making another call as they returned to the car. He disconnected as they reached the vehicle, but didn't speak until they were seated inside it.

He took some bills from his wallet and handed them to her. "That's for my copies."

She stared at the bills, knowing he would refuse to take them back. "That's a dime more than half of what they cost, which puts me in your debt."

He grinned. "Your credit's good."

She squelched a snicker. "Tell me what you learned."

"Mrs. Rathburn is still alive, and she lives in a nursing home in Springfield."

Quincy debated. Did she want to go directly there or to that Country Cuzzins theater first? "Can we go there now?" she asked, reaching a quick decision. Surely a family member would be more informative than whatever they could learn at the theater.

"We can." He started the motor.

Neither of them spoke much during the drive to Springfield, each lost in private thoughts and speculations. But Quincy was very much aware of Delton's presence beside her. And had trouble keeping her eyes from straying to him.

When they arrived at the nursing home and entered the single storied, red brick building, they found themselves in a front lobby that extended across the width of the room. A sofa and a couple of overstuffed chairs sat in front of a low partition, behind which was a spacious dining room. Quincy approached the reception desk at the doorway to their left and spoke to the nurse on duty. "Where would we find Mrs. Jocelyn Rathburn?"

"She lives in room sixty-two, but she's out front right now." The nurse pointed back across the lobby they had just crossed, where two women in wheelchairs sat staring at a large screen television with a newscast blaring. "She's the one on the left."

"Thank you." Quincy walked back that way, Delton keeping pace beside her.

"Mrs. Rathburn?" she said quietly, leaning down near the woman's shoulder.

The woman looked up, her face pale beneath thin white hair that fell in wisps around it. One side of that face sagged in what Quincy guessed to be stroke damage. The woman's eyes narrowed as she studied them, her expression solemn.

Quincy pulled a chair over next to her and sat on it, staring back at the woman, looking for similarities to the news photo in her purse. "Hello, Mrs. Rathburn," she repeated softly, hoping to put the woman at ease. "My name is Quincy Clark, and I'd like to chat with you for a bit if you don't mind."

Mrs. Rathburn's eyes rounded as Quincy stated her name, and then she studied her in puzzlement. An unsteady hand raised to Quincy's cheek, tears forming in the corners of her eyes. "Are you Janet's Quincy?" she asked, her speech a bit slurred but understandable.

"I don't know," Quincy said honestly. "I'm trying to find out who gave birth to me. I'm adopted and have been looking for my birth parents for a long time. I found a newspaper article that mentioned your name."

The woman's hand went over her mouth as Quincy opened her purse and extracted her copy of the article. "Is that you?" She placed it in Mrs. Rathburn's thin veined hand that didn't appear to have any stroke damage. Neither of them paid attention to Delton as he pulled a chair next to Quincy and perched on it.

Jocelyn Rathburn looked down—and sobbed when she saw the picture. "That's my si…sister," she said, choking the words from behind her hand.

"Do you know where she is?" Quincy asked, holding her breath.

She jerked her head back and forth. "I've done ev…everything I could think of to find her. Are you Quincy Jo?"

"I think that's possible, except I didn't know about the Jo part." She managed a weak smile. "What can you tell me about your sister?"

Jocelyn leaned her head back, drinking in the sight of Quincy, her lips quivering. "She loved you. And I thought you were …were gone …like her."

"How long ago did my parents disappear?"

"Twenty-five years," she stammered in a near whisper. "But I don't know exactly when it happened …or what happened. I just …just know that when I …I hadn't heard from Jan in several days, I called her and got no answer. I kept calling. When I didn't hear from her after sev…several calls, we—my husband and I—drove to Branson to see her." She paused in her slow, halting speech to get her breath.

"What did you find?" Delton asked after she had time to relax a bit.

Jocelyn looked at him for the first time. "Who are you?"

"I'm Delton Booker, a detective who's looking into the case."

She inhaled sharply and looked upward. "Oh, thank You, Lord." Then she directed her gaze back at him. "We found an empty house. A neighbor we …spoke to said she saw a moving van loading fur …furniture, figured their neighbors had moved, and thought no more about it."

"What about since then?" Quincy asked. "You never heard from the Claytons again?"

Her head shook. "No. It's been twenty-five years, and …and I've never found out anything about them." She paused. "I know something terrible must have happened, but I can't …can't figure out what it was."

"Who owns the house now?" Delton asked.

Jocelyn's expression turned even sadder. "They still do. Or I do. I don't know. Dave and I …kept hoping …they would return, but they never did. Even after I reported them missing. We started pay …paying the taxes on the house so …so they wouldn't lose it. Then we rented it so we could …make the mortgage payments. Dave took care of them, and it was eventually paid off completely."

"Where is it located?"

Her mouth twisted with the effort to speak. "It's near Hollister." When she quoted an address and directions, Delton made a note.

Out of breath again, Mrs. Rathburn paused. Then she made a motion with her hands. "As time passed, the stress built up so …so much it …caused …me to …to have a stroke."

Quincy's heart broke for the woman who surely had to be her aunt. "How long have you lived here in this facility?"

"Only a …couple of years," she said, wiping at her eyes. "Dave took care of me all those years. Then he died. My son and …daughter each wanted me to live with them. But I chose this."

"You wanted them to concentrate on their own

families," Quincy said, understanding that Jocelyn hadn't wanted to be a burden to them. And probably wouldn't have been, seeing what kind of woman she was. But she hadn't wanted to risk it. Quincy swallowed the lump in her throat, vowing not to forget this sweet lady—to visit her as much as possible.

"I don't know if you know it, but your daughter did something to help you search for your sister," Quincy said, hoping to provide a measure of comfort. "She submitted her DNA to a registry where I submitted mine when I decided to look for my birth family. That's how I found my parents' names and decided to spend the summer in Branson looking for them."

That brought more tears, but clearly ones of joy.

"Mrs. Rathburn," Delton said, compassion in his voice, "I can see that this is tiring for you. May I ask a few more questions, but phrase them so you can answer with a simple yes or no, or a head nod or shake?"

"Of c …course," she agreed, placing a thin hand over his briefly.

"Was it about six weeks after you couldn't reach them that you reported them missing?"

Her head nodded jerkily.

"Your sister was twenty-nine, her husband thirty-one at that time. Is that right?"

Again, she nodded.

So, they would have been fifty-four and fifty-six now, Quincy calculated silently.

Delton cleared his throat before the next question. "Do you think they're alive?"

Jocelyn's face twisted in pain. "No. Please find out what happened to them."

"We're going to do our best," he promised.

"I have one more question," Quincy said. "Did they just work at the theater in that picture, or did they own it?"

"Owned …it," Jocelyn said with difficulty. "With the

…the …other couple."

Quincy stood, leaned over, and hugged the woman. "May I come visit you again?"

"Yes. Oh, yes, please," she repeated, clinging to her.

Chapter 3

Delton glanced over at Quincy as he drove back to Branson. She was clearly having a difficult time emotionally. He couldn't blame her.

"Do you have any theories about what happened to them?" he asked quietly, not wanting to upset her, but needing to hear her thoughts. Something about her tugged at him, something more than a mere desire to help find her parents.

She drew a deep breath. "I agree with Jocelyn. There's no way they're still alive after all this time. I have no idea where they could have gone, or why they didn't take me with them. But I need to know."

"I've read back over that file," he said, wanting to assure her of his sincere desire to solve the case. "The last time anyone reported seeing them was at dinner following the afternoon show at the theater on July the twentieth of the year they disappeared. By the time they were reported missing weeks later, the story didn't garner a lot of attention. People the police talked to reported they had moved, but admitted having no idea they had planned to do so."

"What about their show?"

"They were replaced, but attendance flagged after that.

The theater shut down and then sold only a few months later. It isn't mentioned in the file after that."

She frowned. "I suppose there are always plenty of musicians around, waiting for their big chance. Maybe they hired someone with no name recognition, and it flopped. To me that would seem an indication that the Claytons were much better performers."

Her wan smile wrenched his heart, but he liked her effort to put a positive spin on it.

"Were the partners who stayed at the theater questioned?" she asked.

"Of course. According to the detective's notes, the Ramsey couple said the Claytons weren't happy with the show, were having marital trouble, and moved out of state, leaving them in a financial bind as well as hurting from the loss of their popular musicians."

Quincy frowned at that. "What about the Corvette shown in that news picture? Which couple owned it?"

"It belonged to the Claytons."

"I wonder if anyone at the license office can tell us anything, like if the license was transferred to another state."

"That's something I should have asked Mrs. Rathburn. She might have known the answer." He glanced at the time on the dashboard. "It's lunch time. Why don't we grab a bite to eat and then go there? It won't hurt to check."

Quincy brightened a bit. "Do you think we could also go see the house where they lived? And maybe visit that theater?"

"I think we'll have enough time to do all that. There's a nice burger joint not far from the neighborhood where that house is located. Let's eat there, look at the house and theater, and then go to the courthouse. The county seat is only a few miles away."

Within minutes, they arrived at the eating place, and lunch was a quick affair.

~

They were silent on the drive to locate the house where her parents had lived. Quincy's hands clenched in her lap as Delton turned off the main thoroughfare onto a road that wound through a subdivision populated by a wide variety of home styles and sizes.

He pulled to a stop before a large estate at the end of the road. Surrounded by beautiful landscaping and trees, the hills rose sharply toward a pale blue sky behind it.

As they sat taking in the sight, a woman emerged onto the front porch of the house.

"Let's speak to her." Quincy pushed the car door open and hopped to the ground.

As they walked up the sidewalk, the woman moved down the steps to meet them. "May I help you?"

Quincy guessed her to be in her late forties or early fifties. She had an athletic build and skin that looked as if she might spend a good deal of time at the nearby golf course. A softly rounded face was topped by blond hair cut in a short, spiky bob.

"I just wanted to see this property," Quincy explained forthrightly. "We visited with Jocelyn Rathburn, and she told us she owns it."

The woman's expression turned to one of shrewd appraisal. "Why would she tell you that?"

"I'm trying to find out what happened to my parents. They're the actual owners, or they were. Mrs. Rathburn is my mother's sister."

The woman's slightly frosty expression melted into one of astonishment. "Are you talking about the couple Jocelyn said disappeared?"

Quincy nodded, glancing at Delton. He seemed fine with her leading the conversation—and being so direct.

"I grew up here and remember attending the show at the Country Cuzzins Theater when I was a teenager," the woman volunteered. "But I had no idea until we were looking for a home to buy or rent and found this one listed that it had belonged to them. Mrs. Rathburn wouldn't sell it to us, said she wanted to keep it in case her sister ever returned or was found. My husband and I loved it, so we decided to rent it for a while. That was over ten years ago, and we're still here."

"Have you heard anyone, like neighbors, say what they think happened to Drake and Janet Clayton, or what might have happened to them?" Delton asked.

"The woman next door—she's a widow now, but she and her husband lived here back then—said she saw a moving van and crew show up here one day. They loaded up everything and hauled it away, but she never heard where the Claytons went or anything about them. She had no idea they were planning to leave and was totally shocked by it."

"Did someone else move into the house right away?"

The woman's brow furrowed, her head shaking slowly. "No-o-o. I believe she said the place was vacant for a long time. Then Mrs. Rathburn showed up one day asking about her sister. The house was still empty for some time after that, but eventually someone moved into it. They were the only tenants before us."

"Is there anything more you can tell us?" Delton prodded when she hesitated.

Her mouth did a little twist. "I don't want to say anything negative."

"Look," Quincy cut back into the conversation. "I just want to find them. If you know anything else at all, please tell us."

"Well," she began, but hesitated another moment before continuing. "I understand there were rumors of trouble in the marriage, one of them had an affair or something. I never heard any details and didn't pay much attention. Rumors always happen. You know that."

Quincy nodded. "You're right. Thank you for your time."

~

"I don't believe they're alive," Delton commented as he drove back to town. "So I wonder what happened to their furniture and personal belongings."

Quincy stared forward. "I don't know, but someone around here does."

"And they don't want you to find out." He knew she referred to that attack. "We'll keep digging, and retracing the old investigation, until we know the full truth."

When they arrived at the license office, they had to stand in line behind two individuals. Once at the counter, Delton showed his badge and explained to the clerk that they wanted to know if the Clayton vehicle title to the red Corvette had ever been transferred. After a wait while she checked, they were told that without a VIN number she was unable to locate any records relating to the car. But she was able to tell them that neither of the Claytons had ever renewed or transferred their driver's licenses.

"Well, we knew it was a long shot," Quincy said as they headed back to the car.

"Let's hope for better luck at the theater." He clicked the button to unlock the car doors.

The theater now known as the Heartland Hoedown had a bright neon sign of its name displayed over the top of the arched entryway. Although the parking lot was nearly empty, the front door was unlocked. Inside, they found a cleaning crew, either tidying up after a show or in preparation for one—or both.

"May we speak to the manager or owner?" Delton asked, showing his badge to the middle-aged woman working near the ticket booth.

She put her cleaning cloth on her cart. "I'll see if he's in his office. Wait here."

They watched the woman go to a door at one end of the lobby, tap on it, and step inside. Moments later she emerged. "He said come on in."

As she returned to her duties, they entered the office,

where a middle-aged, dark haired—likely chemically enhanced—man stood and extended a hand across his desk. His gaze darted from one to the other of them. "How may I help you?" His speech was cool and cultured.

Quincy shook the man's hand briefly, and then watched as Delton shook it more firmly. "We're looking for information about this theater. I'm afraid I don't know your name," Delton apologized while showing his badge. "We saw a picture of this theater in an old newspaper story, and it raised some questions."

"I'm Garth Carruthers," the man said, a cautious note in his voice as he resumed his seat. "And I can't imagine what questions you have."

"How long have you owned the property?"

The man frowned, but he answered. "I purchased it over twenty years ago, and the paperwork was handled by my attorney." He leaned back and laced his fingers together over his expensive suit. A huge gold ring glittered on his right hand, an emerald one from the left hand. The scent of spicy cologne drifting from him was overpowering. Everything about him shouted money and self-importance.

"I'd like to know who owned it before you, if you don't mind telling us."

His eyes narrowed. "I don't see what business it is to the police, especially after all this time, but I bought it from a couple by the name of Ramsey. If I remember correctly, their names were Allen and Sharleen."

"Only one couple owned it?"

The man's face went blank. A finger tapped on the desktop, making the ring flash. Then a glimmer of understanding replaced the blankness. "Yes, it was one couple. They said they had bought out their partners' interest in the place. That's what you wanted to know, right?"

Delton nodded. "Did they say why the partners sold out to them?"

Mr. Carruthers stared up at the ceiling for a moment,

lost in thought. Then he looked back at Delton. "That was a long time ago, but I recall them saying the other couple had problems, were tired of the business, and had left the area. They also said it left them in a difficult position. I never met the other couple personally, and the Ramsey couple had been the sole owners for some time before selling it. They were struggling financially, and the new performers they hired hadn't worked out. They said they had to get out from under the stress."

It wasn't much, but it was a trail to follow. Delton thanked Mr. Carruthers for his time and they left.

Once back in the car, he pulled out his phone. "I want to know more about the Ramsey couple," he explained to Quincy.

She reached for her phone as well. "Me, too."

They both began hitting search engines, but Delton had police resources not available to her and came up with an interesting fact before Quincy could find anything. "The Ramsey couple divorced not long after selling their business," he informed her.

"Well, they both dropped out of sight after that," she said, sounding frustrated. "They're not on any social media that I can find, and I can't locate any news about them since the sale. They must have left show business altogether."

He agreed. "Okay, let's visit the courthouse and see if we can find out anything about that theater deed."

As they put their phones away, he saw Quincy's head turn, as if searching for something behind them. "What's wrong?"

She took several moments before facing him. "I'm being paranoid."

"I guess I am, too," he admitted, scanning the streets. "Do you have an itchy feeling that we're being followed?"

She nodded. "I think I saw the same gray van parked down the street that I noticed at the edge of the parking lot when we came out of the theater."

He started the motor. "Let's go on to the Recorder of Deeds office, but keep our eyes open for that vehicle."

Neither of them noted such a van following them during the twenty-minute drive to Forsyth. He parked near the courthouse, and they went inside. When they located the recorder's office and approached the customer service counter, Delton again showed his badge, hoping for quick cooperation. "I'd like to examine the history of the deed to the Heartland Hoedown Theater."

The middle-aged clerk tipped her head, her expression a mixture of puzzlement and concern. "I can tell you without looking that it's been in the possession of Mr. Carruthers for at least twenty years."

"I want to be sure there wasn't anything wrong with that deed when he bought it. I'm not looking to cause trouble for the man. I just need some information."

"Okay. Can you give me a few minutes to do a search?"

"We'll wait." He faced Quincy. "Would you prefer to wait in the car or in here?"

"In here."

As soon as they took the seats she indicated, they each returned to their phones and internet browsing, needing something to do and in unspoken agreement that they didn't want to discuss the matter in the presence of other people.

Several minutes later, the clerk returned to the counter, her expression somber. She beckoned, and then spoke quietly when they approached. "The transaction between Mr. Carruthers and the Ramsey couple seems fine, but I believe there's a problem with the transfer of the property to the Ramseys from the Claytons."

Delton frowned. "Are you saying the signature isn't authentic?"

Her head bobbed jerkily. "I didn't work here back when this was dated." She placed the document on the counter for them to see. "But I'm afraid it was forged, and then sold to an innocent third party. I found where the two couples originally purchased it, but the Clayton signature on that one doesn't match the one on the later document."

Delton placed a hand on the document. "Is this copy for us?"

The clerk nodded. He took it, thanked her, and accompanied Quincy out of the office.

At the car, he sat motionless behind the wheel, his mental wheels turning. After several moments, he faced her. "I don't know what happened back then, or is happening right now. But here's what I want you to do."

She waited for him to explain.

"I'm going to take you back to your camper and watch you go inside. Then I'm going to drive away, as if I'm leaving. But I'll park out of sight and return on foot to watch in case anyone comes lurking around."

Chapter 4

Quincy crawled into bed, so tired she assumed she would fall asleep immediately. But she didn't. Instead, she stared up at the ceiling in the dark, the events of the last two days replaying over and over in her mind.

A sound caught her ear. She strained to hear. Was she being paranoid?

She tensed as another sound reached her. Easing out of bed, she pushed back the side of the curtain, and peered out the window. The sight of a dark shadow near a tree made her breath catch. She leaned forward, straining in an effort to make out any features. The hair on the back of her neck stood on end.

She started to go for her phone to call Delton, but hesitated when she caught a fleeting glimpse of another dark figure moving around behind the first one. She waited, hardly able to breathe.

Suddenly the first figure darted away from the tree and started across the section of campground, clearly headed for her camper. But then the second figure, one she was sure by now was Delton, charged forward and took the first person to the ground.

As they wrestled, Quincy grabbed her robe and ran to

the front room of the camper, pulling the robe around her as she moved. She grabbed the big, long handled flashlight from the counter, turned it on, and stepped out onto the ground.

As she flashed the beam over the struggling figures, the one she now confirmed was Delton landed a solid jab at the other one's jaw. Momentarily stunned, the intruder twisted away and stumbled to his feet.

Quincy ran toward them, shining the flashlight in the intruder's ski mask concealed face. He jerked his head aside but landed a kick at Delton, knocking him back to the ground from his half risen position. Then the masked intruder whirled and took off at a dead run. Moments later, a motor sounded, and then a motorcycle could be heard roaring away.

Delton gained his footing and hurried to where Quincy stood. "You can't stay here. It's too accessible. You have to find another place to stay."

She glanced around the campground, taking in the proximity of other campers and realizing that, whether she wanted to leave or not, she shouldn't put these other people at risk.

"I'm not sure where that would be."

He pulled out his phone. "Let me call my friend."

"I hate to abandon Dad's camper."

"I'll ask Logan if we can park it in his back yard. He has a privacy fence. The camper would be concealed inside it."

"I don't have any better ideas," she admitted, listening as he made the call and wishing she could hear the other side of the conversation.

He disconnected and faced her. "Logan said we can park your camper in his yard. He's a friend I worked summers and became good friends with when we were both in high school. Now he's the tech guru on the police force here. I'm staying with him and his wife while I'm filling in for their detective who's out with an injury. After we get the camper moved, I'll take you to the hotel where Ginger and Erin are, and you can stay with them."

She grimaced. "I don't want to intrude on your friends."

"You won't. They'll be happy for your company."

Quincy drew a deep breath and bowed to the inevitable. "Okay, I'll go to the hotel, but I'll get my own room near your friends."

It didn't take long to hitch the camper to the van, and then drive, with Delton keeping close to her bumper, to a home in a nice neighborhood. No one was home, the friend and his wife both at work while their kids were at day care.

Delton waited while Quincy packed a few clothes, and then he followed her to the hotel. They parked and entered the building together, but Quincy forged ahead to the desk and asked for a single room.

"She'd like to be as near our friends as possible. They're in room four-twenty-three," Delton interjected, stepping up beside her at the counter.

The clerk studied her computer screen. "I have a room two doors down the hall from them. Will that do?"

Quincy nodded. "That's fine." It would be near his friends, but far enough away to give her some space. She was thankful for the safe haven, but couldn't forget that someone, she had no idea who, was out to kill her.

~

Delton polished off the last of his omelet and picked up his coffee cup, having arrived in time to meet Quincy and his friends for breakfast in the hotel dining area. He had slept reasonably well after getting Quincy moved out of that campground and into this place near the two couples.

His pulse quickened at the sight of Quincy seated at the end of the table directly to his left. He had never been instantly drawn to someone this way. Maybe he was losing it. *Keep your head on straight, Bud.*

She raised her head, a cautious expression on her face. "I really need to go to work today. I know you said I should stay here, but they're shorthanded at the Homestead this week and really need me. I just couldn't bring myself to call and tell them I can't make it."

He hesitated to answer, but understood her position. "Whoever is after you knows what kind of vehicle you drive. Leave it parked behind Logan's house, and I'll take you. I'm going to spend the day with you. I've already called my captain and gotten his approval." He had expected this.

She nodded agreement, but he could tell she wasn't thrilled about it. He couldn't blame her for not wanting to be without her own vehicle, but she apparently recognized that he was right and didn't argue about it.

As soon as the meal was finished, they left the table and went to his pickup, having decided to drive it rather than a police car today—and dressing in jeans and a short-sleeved powder blue shirt rather than his more business-like attire. He glanced over at her as they buckled their seat belts, and their gazes locked. His gut clenched, making him forget that he shouldn't be so attracted to her. He'd accepted that marriage and family wouldn't work for him.

"Do very many people know you're searching for your birth parents?" he asked, needing to get his brain back on track.

A thoughtful frown crossed her face. "I haven't made a secret of it, but I haven't broadcast it openly either."

He started the engine and drove into the street. "You've indicated your dad knows. Do you know if he has discussed it with others?"

"I doubt it, but I don't know. He makes a lot of contacts when he's working on something, whether it's job related or personal, so he could have."

"What about you? Who have you told?"

She shrugged. "I've been to the newspaper office and courthouse with you and spoken to employees at each. Then there was the theater owner, and the clerk at the recorder's office."

"What about at work? Have you talked about your search with co-workers or supervisors?"

She shook her head. "I've only been here a couple of weeks, and I've been too busy to form any close friendships. The only persons I've connected with on a personal level are Ginger and Erin and their fiancés. And we both know they're not after me. Did you get a look at that intruder's face last night?"

"I didn't see a face, but I made note of a few things. I'm quite sure it was a guy. He was approximately six feet tall, with a lanky build and narrow shoulders. His head was covered by a ski mask."

"Someone apparently doesn't want me finding out the truth, but he's only making me more certain that it needs to be uncovered."

She was right. He just hated for her to be exposed to such potential danger. He drove in silence to the Homestead parking lot, parked, and faced her. He read agitation and determination in the set of her jaw and the gleam in her eye. "I understand your position, but I don't want to see you hurt. Please let me do my job and protect you."

Her hands clenched and unclenched, but she met his gaze without flinching. "I get that you have a job to do— even that you want to protect me. But I don't think you understand my motives. I want to know why I was abandoned."

He heaved a deep breath. "I know a little something about abandonment. My dad left my mother and me when I was four." He didn't go any farther into his past, but he saw a glimmer of empathy enter the depths of her eyes.

She glanced at her watch. "I need to get going."

Delton hadn't expected to enjoy the day, but found the tour, as well as the guide, both interesting and informative. He rode in the passenger seat beside Quincy in the Jeep after she greeted tourists and assisted those who needed it onto the wagon-like tram with a roof-like cover over it. He was impressed with her communication skills as she drove along the mountainous trail and shared interesting facts about the different landmarks that included visits to Old Matt's cabin, Inspiration Point that had been erected in honor of the author of the book The Shepherd of the Hills, as well as the site of Old Matt's grist mill and Jennings' Still and the Morgan Community Church. The tour was a history lesson designed to set the stage for the evening performance of the play at the huge outdoor theater.

"You must be a very good teacher," he commented as she scooted behind the wheel for the last tour at four o'clock. "You know your subject and share the knowledge in ways that keep your listeners interested. And you do a nice blend of educator, host and escort. Your classes must be popular with the students."

She kept her attention focused ahead and put the Jeep into motion, apparently uncomfortable at the compliment. "My evaluations are good, but I enjoy what I do. What about you? Do you like your job?"

Once again, she had diverted the subject. He grinned. "It's what I chose to do, and I get satisfaction from providing answers and safety for citizens who need it. But I don't think I'm the level of over-achiever you are."

She darted a sideways frown over at him. "What do you mean?"

"I suspect that you have a tendency to push harder, do more, because you harbor some insecurity from thinking you were abandoned. So you tend to always be proving yourself."

She shot him another glance, this one a glare. "How would you know such a thing? It sounds to me like you're diagnosing yourself."

He shrugged, scanning the terrain. The hardest part of the day had been remembering that there could be someone out there looking for an opportunity to hurt her—or worse—and being constantly on the alert. "I may have been accused of such a thing and sensed a kinship with you."

Her glare cleared away, to be replaced by a twitch at the corners of her mouth. "How about we agree that we chose our careers and like them—and let it go at that?"

He let it go. But his brain continued humming as she repeated her final tour and spiel of the day. No, he hadn't been abandoned at birth, but his dad had left and never kept in touch with them. His mother had worked long hours and left him and his sister on their own a lot—too much as he grew older. Darlene had been a good kid, but as a teen Delton had begun hanging out with the wrong crowd.

Getting arrested for participating in a wild party had been the result, but had also been a turning point. No charges had been made, but it had shocked his mother into recognizing his downward spiral in behavior so much that she had changed her own ways, become more available, observant and helpful. Together they had established a better relationship and even begun attending church.

He had found friends among the church youth and broken away from the friends who had been headed for trouble. He wasn't sure how much trust he placed in God, but the church involvement had definitely been a good thing.

His thoughts rushed back to Quincy. Apparently, she had a much stronger relationship with God, which led him to think she might have ended up being raised in better circumstances than she would have had with her birth parents.

A vision of the Clayton estate came to mind. And that in turn brought remembrance of a particular case in the department's files. A rich couple had been searching for the baby stolen from them as an infant, and when the fact became public, people had come from near and far claiming to be that child, hoping to become rich.

Could Quincy be trying to work a scheme like that?

His gut said it was possible. His heart said no. But his cop training said he had to consider all angles.

When her shift ended and she had signed off duty, they headed for his pickup. As he opened the door and slid behind the wheel, movement near the exit of the parking lot caught his attention. A second later the sharp crack of gunfire split the air, and glass shattered from the passenger window.

He lunged toward Quincy, swung his arm across her glass covered shoulders, and shoved. "Get down!"

Another crack sounded, this one the thud and ping of a bullet ricocheting off the bumper.

Chapter 5

"**Get down**," Delton repeated, pressing Quincy's head to her lap.

Adrenalin pumping wildly through her veins, she gasped for breath and tried to gather her incoherent thoughts. All she could grasp was that there was no longer any doubt that someone was out to kill her.

He rammed a key into the ignition, cranked the engine, and hit the gas pedal. As the vehicle shot forward, he said, "Call 911. Tell them shots were fired at us in the Homestead parking lot and we're hitting the street to get out of range."

"Keep driving. We're on the way," a voice responded as she finished.

Delton glanced over at Quincy. "Are you all right?"

She nodded, the motion doing nothing positive for the ringing in her ears. But she did turn to look behind them. "I don't see any vehicle that looks like it's following us."

"The shots probably drew enough attention that the shooter had to focus on getting out of there rather than coming after us. I'd better drive to the station."

Quincy soon found herself seated in a room with Delton, facing his chief and another officer. Their questioning, probably in deference to Delton, was polite and not intimidating. Once they were satisfied that they had the complete picture of what had been happening, she and Delton were allowed to leave.

"I don't think the shooter realized I'm a cop," Delton said as they returned to his vehicle.

She nodded. "I agree." His lack of uniform and driving his own vehicle had hidden that fact.

"I think the fact that he risked shooting at you in such a busy place means he hasn't found your camper, but I think you should stay with Erin and Ginger tonight. Then I'll take you somewhere else tomorrow, since I think they're checking out and going home at the end of the week."

Quincy didn't have any better idea, so she kept silent as he drove to the hotel. The room she had vacated earlier was still vacant, so she reclaimed it.

"Is the room next to her available?" Delton asked the clerk.

She checked. "Yes, it is. Last night's guests left late, and the maids just finished cleaning it."

"I'll take it."

Quincy didn't question him until he had registered and been given a key. "Why did you do that?" she asked when they were in the elevator, him carrying her bag that they had stopped by the Fuller house and retrieved from her car.

"I think I need to stick close to you, and it might be an opportunity to visit with friends."

She couldn't argue with that, at least the second part.

When they reached the fourth floor, they put her bag in her room and went down the hall. But when Delton knocked on Erin and Ginger's door, no one answered.

He faced Quincy. "I guess they've already gone to eat. I'd suggest we do the same, but someone could have followed us and be watching for you. How about we place an order with room service and eat in one of our rooms?"

She made for her own room. Once inside, they checked the menus they found next to the television and placed orders, a chef salad for her and a steak sandwich for him.

"What do you do with your time when you're not teaching school or working a summer job?' he asked, turning from opening the blinds and peering out into the daylight that was just starting to fade.

She moved from the hard chair to the side of the bed. "Well, I used to attend church and school functions with mother, and I went camping and to Cardinal baseball games with both parents. In the two years since Mom's death, Dad and I have gone camping once or twice each summer."

He pulled a chair away from the desk, turned it backward, and sat facing her with his arms braced on the chair back. "What about friends?"

She placed a pillow behind her spine and eased back against the headboard. "A fellow teacher and I hang out together a lot."

"A guy?" he asked after a moment of scrutiny.

"Corey's the business teacher, and she's a few years older than me. Her twelve-year-old daughter is in the Sunday School class I teach."

"Isn't there a special someone in your life?"

"You mean a man, don't you?"

A flicker of a smile crossed his face. "That's what I mean."

She shrugged. "I date some. I'm not a recluse. But I'm not serious about anyone. I guess I need to find out who and what I am before I can think about anyone that way." No relationships had ever seemed interesting enough to become more important than her job, and then this search for her roots. But she had seen enough bad relationships to make her think men were just too much trouble. "What about you? Is there a significant person in your life?"

"No wife. No girlfriend."

Quincy experienced a flash of relief, which was ridiculous. She wasn't looking for entanglements. And the shuttered look on his face said the subject had just closed.

A knock at the door signaled arrival of their food. She grabbed her purse and made it there first. But when she reached for her wallet, Delton edged between her and the delivery person. "This one's on me. You've already fed me twice."

He had her there, so she took the order while he paid for it. Once the staff member was gone, they went back to their seats and ate with minimal conversation.

"Don't open this door to anyone but me," Delton instructed as he opened it. "I'll take you to work again in the morning."

"Thank you. Sleep well."

He gave her a half grin and went to his room.

~

The next morning, Quincy and Delton had just returned to her hotel room from breakfast when her phone rang. It was her dad. "Hey, old man," she greeted him.

A sharp journalist, Gary Clark might be confined to a wheelchair, but he still worked for his newspaper—mostly from home. His mind was still acute, he was extremely savvy, and he drove a wheelchair accessible van.

"How's it going?" he asked, ignoring the lighthearted jibe at his age.

She didn't want to tell him about the attacks, but he'd find out. "It seems that someone doesn't like me asking questions about the Claytons. I was jumped after work." She explained about the near strangling and being shot at later.

Gary whistled. "Something's downright nasty about this. Maybe you should come home and let me hire a private investigator to find out what's behind it."

"The police have a detective on it," she said before he could continue outlining a plan. "Have you dug up any new information yet?"

"I have. And that detective needs to hear it. Is he there?"

"Yes, he is."

"Let me talk to him."

Quincy blinked. It sounded like Gary had something important, but he wanted to check out the detective. She placed her hand over the phone and directed her gaze at Delton. "My dad wants to talk to you."

He made a little mouth shrug and took the phone. "Hello, Sir. How may I help you?"

Quincy watched as Delton listened to whatever her dad said. His responses were minimal in exchanging introductions, and then his expression morphed from casual to intense. At one point he yanked a notepad from his pocket and jotted a note on it.

"Thank you, Sir," he said before disconnecting.

"Well, did he read you the riot act about taking care of me?" she asked.

He produced a slight grin. "I guess you might call it that. But it smacked of a father's love. He said he'll call you again later, when you're alone and more relaxed."

"He said he had information. What was it?"

Delton's eyes narrowed. "He said he discovered that your birth dad had two brothers. They were more traceable than possible sisters because their last name was Clayton. One DNA trail led to an obituary of the brother named Dean, who died of cancer when he was in his forties. There were no children, but there's a widow. Her name is Opal, and she lives in Little Rock. Gary called her, and she said she hadn't seen much of your parents before they disappeared, seeing that they lived over a hundred miles apart. Then, after her husband got sick, she was caught up in taking care of Dean, and then losing him. She said she felt bad that she hadn't done more about locating Drake and Janet, but she had always wondered what happened to them."

Discouragement seeped through Quincy as Delton shared her dad's findings—until he continued.

"Before the conversation ended, your dad learned from the widow that her brother-in-law is alive and has a daughter. He even got her to give him an address and phone number for them. I'm impressed with your dad's research. What kind of work does he do when he's not researching your lost history?"

She grinned. "He's a journalist, and he's good. He's extremely computer savvy and has the tenacity of a bulldog. He also has an arsenal of resources."

"So his information should be solid. Good. Do you want to go see your surviving uncle? He lives in Reed Springs, which is only about a half hour from here. We could go as soon as you finish your work shift and get something to eat along the way."

It didn't take any time for Quincy to decide. "I came here to find my parents, not to have a good time or make a living. I want to talk to anyone who can tell me what happened to them and why they didn't take me with them. I'm scheduled to work tomorrow, but not today, so we can go right now."

It only took thirty minutes to drive to Reed Springs and locate the address her dad had given Delton. He turned onto a long, paved driveway and parked before a large frame house with a porch across the entire front of it.

She exited the vehicle and stood for a moment, staring at the large home occupied by an unknown relative. She remained silent as Delton escorted her onto the porch and rang the doorbell.

The gentleman who opened the door looked to be in his late fifties. His hair was still dark around the edges, but white on top. He frowned. "Yes?"

"My name is Quincy Clark," she spoke up promptly, "and this is Detective Delton Booker. May we come in and chat with you?"

"What about?"

Quincy gulped. "Your family …that I think is my family."

His rounded eyes signaled an inner jaw drop. He opened the door wider and motioned them inside and to seats facing the overstuffed chair he practically fell onto. He stared at Quincy. "Explain what you mean."

She took a deep breath. "First I need to ask a question. Are you the brother of Dean and Drake Clayton?"

"Yeeees," he said slowly, clearly not assimilating. "But I'm the only one still living, so far as I know," he added a little more steadily.

"Quincy is searching for her birth family," Delton cut into the conversation. "She thinks she's the daughter of your brother, Drake."

The man gasped, his face going pale. He leaned forward. "Quincy?" he repeated, studying her in stunned amazement.

Quincy nodded. "I was adopted when I was almost two years old. My parents told me about it when I was eight, but it was only after my mother died that my dad encouraged me to search for my birth parents and satisfy my curiosity about where I came from and why I was given away."

He rubbed a hand over his face. "How can that be? Drake and Janet have been gone so long that everyone, including me, just assumed something bad happened to them and you."

"That's what I'm trying to find out. Did they give me away, or did someone do something to them and take me from them? All I have at this point is questions. The most connections I've found are a woman who is my mother's sister—and now you."

"Tell me everything you've done," he said, his voice quavering. "You look a little like your mother."

She explained about the DNA database and all that had led her to him. "My search has apparently touched a hot wire," she said when finished. "Someone has attacked me at my workplace, and then shot at me later."

"That makes me agree with you that something bad happened to your brother and his wife," Delton said when she paused.

Don Clayton's body shook. "Do you think you can find out what it was, and who did it?"

"We're going to do our best," Delton assured him.

"Do you have any pictures of them?" Quincy asked.

He became thoughtful. "My wife kept an album, but I'm not sure where it is. I'll hunt for it and call you if I find it— if you'll give me a phone number."

She whipped out a pen and piece of paper from her purse and jotted it down for him. "Thank you so much, Don. Is it okay if I call you that?"

He smiled. "It is, but I think Uncle Don would sound better."

She returned the smile, happily surprised at his ready acceptance of her claim of kinship.

"I wish my wife could have met you," he said in a wistful tone. "She battled cancer for a long time. I lost her two years ago. Our daughter is only a few years older than you and loved playing with you when you were tiny. She thought you were her dolly. Over the years she has wondered about you and talked about you."

"What about my dad?" Quincy asked. "Do you have any idea what could have happened to your brother?"

Don's head rotated slowly back and forth, his expression sad. "I wish I did. They simply disappeared into thin air. Having you show up here after all this time has me reeling."

"Did you know my parents' business partners?"

He made a noncommittal hand waving motion. "I met them and attended their show a few times, but I didn't know them on a personal level."

"So you don't know if there was any kind of trouble with the business?"

He went motionless, creases etched between his brows. "They never shared business details with me," he said slowly, "but the last time I talked to Drake, he seemed tense. When I asked him if he had a problem, he said he had a tough decision to make. I assumed it was about the business. I wish I could help you more, but I'm clueless."

After Quincy gave Don her phone number and they said their good-byes, he called, "Come again any time," as she and Delton went out the door.

Chapter 6

"What are your thoughts?" Delton asked when they were back in his truck. He started the engine and turned on the air conditioner. The temperature was already near eighty and rising steadily, the weather having turned hotter almost overnight.

"I'm happy at finding another relative," she said while buckling her seat belt, "but it hurts to be so certain that my parents are dead."

"Don seemed happy at meeting you," he said, looking both ways and then pulling into the street. "I think I need to find your parents' former business partners. And I have an idea where you can stay tonight."

She twisted in the seat to face him. "Where?"

"I've been staying in my friend, Logan's, guest room. But you could stay there and let me sleep in your camper in their back yard." It would also be a good setup for surveillance, in case they had been followed there.

She took her time responding. "When could we go see the former partners?"

"Well, Logan and his wife should both be at work, but I can call him now and have him do his search magic. What he finds will determine what's next."

"I don't want to impose on your friends, but the other part sounds good."

"Dana will welcome you, and Logan will want to help protect you. If you'll connect my phone," he indicated the dashboard, "I'll call him now. Put it on speaker." He handed the device to her.

She plugged it in for him, found the number, and dialed.

"Yeah, Del. What's up?"

"I need info on a pair of names. See what you can find on Allen and Sharleen Ramsey, former owners of the Country Cuzzins Theater. I need an address if you can find it."

"I'll call you back soon as I have anything."

Delton thanked him and placed the phone in the cup holder beside him. "If he hasn't called by the time we get to Branson, we'll go to his house so I can change clothes," he said to Quincy.

When he hadn't heard from Logan by the time they reached the outskirts of town, he drove on to the house and parked in his usual spot in the driveway.

"They have an excellent alarm system here," he explained, climbing out of the car and grabbing Quincy's bag from behind the driver's seat. "And your camper suits me fine. It's out of sight from the street and an excellent place for me to keep watch over the place."

She met him at the front of the vehicle. "That's your real motive, isn't it?"

"It's *a* motive," he said, glad she seemed okay with the arrangement.

He grasped her arm lightly and ushered her toward the front door. "I'll show you to your room, pack some clothes for myself, and take them to the camper. I'll change while I'm there."

She paused to face him. "I know it's your job, but thank you for helping me."

"We'll get to the bottom of this," he assured her. "Relax

for a few minutes, and I'll let you know when I'm ready for whatever's next."

His phone rang as he finished the sentence. It was Logan.

"The Ramsey couple divorced years ago. I've found an address for him, but not her. She could have remarried and changed her name."

"Give me the one you have." He jotted it on his hand with a pen he snatched from the foyer table at the front of the stairs. "Thanks. We're at your place now, but we'll go look for this guy in a few minutes."

"Make yourself at home. Dana and the kids will be home before me. She's expecting you. It's the least we can do while you're helping the department this summer. Oops, another line's ringing."

Delton stuffed his phone back in his pocket. "I have Allen Ramsey's address," he told Quincy. "It's in Fayetteville. Let's go."

The two-hour drive gave Delton time to reflect on what his research had told him about Allen Ramsey. According to an old police report he had read, the man had a reputation of being full of self-importance and a domineering employer. There had been a couple of police visits related to disputes that became physical at the theater.

They found the man's current stately home in a new housing development, surrounded by a wrought iron fence. It looked as if he had done well for himself. Delton parked in the driveway, and he and Quincy walked in sync through the gate to the front door.

The man who answered the doorbell was solidly built, with beetle brows, and in his fifties. His white shirt was a bit wilted, but the gray dress pants still held a crease.

His eyes that looked as if they had seen too little sleep narrowed on them. "Who are you?"

"I'm Detective Delton Booker." Delton showed his badge and indicated Quincy. "This is Quincy Clark. We'd like to talk to you for a few minutes."

"What about?" He didn't budge.

"I'm looking for my parents," she spoke up quickly. "They were business partners with you and your wife over twenty years ago."

He stared at her as if seeing a ghost. "What partners?"

"Drake and Janet Clayton," Delton supplied. "May we come inside?"

Mr. Ramsey hesitated a moment, but then stepped back to admit them.

"Can you tell us where the Claytons are?" Delton asked once they were seated on the sofa facing the man.

He had plopped in a large, overstuffed chair, his gaze locked on Quincy. His head rotated back and forth slowly, his focus shifting to Delton. "I have no idea."

"When was the last time you saw them?"

He frowned. "I'm not sure of a date. It was so long ago, over twenty years. I've wondered about them often."

"You spent a lot of time with the couple and worked with them. Did you also have a close personal relationship?"

"Of course, we did," he said, his mouth curved into what seemed a pseudo smile. "We were partners." Then his body language underwent a gentle change, becoming a little more amicable. "We had a good thing going, but they got tired of the business, burned out I guess. They sold their interest in the theater to us and moved away. I think they said they were going to Florida, but they could have gone anywhere."

"I understand your wife also went her own way. Where would I find her?"

He shrugged. "She remarried. The last I knew she and Benny Boy lived in a condo out past the Southern Flicks Drive-In. I guess she likes theaters," he added with a hint of sarcasm. Then he looked at his watch and stood. "I have an appointment in ten minutes."

"What's Benny Boy's last name?"

"Bledsoe," he said, opening the door.

After being practically evicted from the house, Delton and Quincy climbed back into his pickup. He looked over at her. "Did you get the feeling the man was shocked—and is lying?"

She nodded. "I did. I think he had something to do with the disappearance of my parents."

"But we need proof. Let's see if we can find his ex."

It didn't take long to find the condo Mr. Ramsey had indicated. Delton knocked on the door—and got no response. He knocked again. Then he heard movement inside.

An elderly, white-haired woman opened the door and squinted out at them. "May I help you?"

"We're looking for Mr. and Mrs. Benny Bledsoe, and this is the address we were given. Do you know them?"

Her already wrinkled face gained more creases. "No, I don't." She backed away, as if to close the door, but then stopped. She raised a finger. "Wait a minute."

Delton waited while her eyes scanned the sky in deep thought. Then her face brightened. "I remember now. I saw that name on some mail that came when I first moved here over a year ago. I had to talk to the mailman two or three times before their junk mail stopped coming here."

Delton gave her a smile. "Thank you, Ma'am. We won't bother you any longer."

They returned to his truck. "Let's stop as soon as we see a restaurant and eat something."

~

As Delton drove away from the truck stop where they had found a satisfying meal, Quincy said, "I wish we knew more about the Ramseys."

He handed her his phone. "Dial Logan for me, and I'll see what he can find."

She plugged it into the dashboard, dialed, and turned on the speaker. "I was just getting ready to call you," Logan responded on the second ring.

"Does that mean you can tell me more about the Clayton case?" Delton asked, his gaze never deviating from the highway.

"I can. The Clayton and Ramsey couples had one child each, the Claytons a little girl, the Ramseys a boy."

"Yeah, we know about the girl," Delton said, darting a glance over at Quincy. "Tell me about the boy."

"He was several years older than the girl," his friend the tech officer said. "According to what I can find, he was a good kid, but began drinking heavily in his teens. When his parents divorced, he was sent to a private boarding school. I guess they thought he needed more discipline than either of them could manage. Anyhow, he's almost forty now and lives in Rockaway Beach. He's twice divorced, with kids who live with their mothers. He's still a heavy drinker and is estranged from his parents."

"We're on our way back from visiting Mr. Ramsey in Fayetteville," Delton explained. "If you can give us the son's address, we'll stop in Rockaway and look for him."

"Here's where you can look."

Quincy grabbed a pen and pad from her purse and jotted down the address Logan quoted. "Thanks," she said, letting Logan know she was privy to the call.

"I assume this is Quincy?"

"Yes. I hope you don't mind your friend dumping me on you."

"Oh, no. We want you safe and your parents found. I look forward to meeting you in person." His tone sounded cordial and sincere.

"Thank you. I appreciate everything you're doing." She darted a look at Delton that let him know he was included in the sentiment.

"Good luck."

Almost two hours later, Quincy scanned each side of the road as Delton turned onto the main street of Rockaway Beach and cruised slowly along, watching for the street

Logan had named. When he found it, he parked in the lot at the left end of a two-story brick apartment building with a partially enclosed verandah across the front of it. It wasn't in the best condition.

They found the apartment number, and Delton knocked on the door. The man who opened the door was about six foot and dark haired, dressed in worn jeans and a black tee shirt with the sleeves torn out. He peered out at them blankly.

Quincy stared at him, looking for any resemblance to his dad, and not seeing it.

"Whatcha want?" He hiccupped, emitting a powerful alcohol breath.

Delton flashed his badge. "I'm Detective Booker. Are you Sean Ramsey?"

"Yeah."

"May we come in and talk to you?"

He drew back, his expression wary. "You mean they sent a cop after me 'cause I missed work being sick?"

"No, we're not here about your work. We want to ask you about someone you knew when you were a boy."

Sean stared at them through eyes hazy from drink. Then he shrugged and stepped back for them to enter. "Make yourselves at home."

Quincy's gaze scanned the room. Clearly a bachelor's pad, it was sparsely furnished, with a brown leather sofa, a couple of rockers, and a TV. But it was relatively neat, only a few odds and ends lying about. Sean plopped in one of the rockers, picked up the bottle of drink from the coffee table before him, and gulped from it.

Delton took the other rocker and went straight to the point. "Do you remember the people who were business partners with your parents when you were a boy?"

Sean plunked the bottle down, his face crinkled in confusion—or shock. He wiped his mouth with the back of his hand and sat peering into space for several moments before looking back at Delton. "I remember them, but I was just a kid and they were my mom and dad's work partners. I had nothing to do with them."

"They were my parents," Quincy interjected, unable to keep quiet. "They disappeared and haven't been seen or heard from in over twenty-five years. We're trying to find them."

Sean frowned, leaning forward to study her more closely. "I remember they had a baby. Are you saying you were that baby?"

She nodded. "I was. I'm Quincy Clark. I was adopted when I was almost two. Now I'd like to find out why that happened, learn my history."

"All I remember is Mom and Dad saying the Claytons moved away. This is the first time I've heard their names since then. Sorry I can't help you." He lolled back in the chair.

When further questions elicited the same response, Delton stood. So did Quincy. "Thanks. Have a good rest of the day. We'll show ourselves out."

Back in the truck, she buckled her seat belt and twisted around to face him. "He gave me the feeling he's playing dumb, hiding something."

Delton's mouth formed a tight line. "I agree. And I learned a long time ago to not ignore my gut instincts."

~

"This is Quincy Clark," Delton introduced her to Logan as he ushered her inside the front doorway of the Fuller home.

"Come on in here," Logan said, extending a handshake to her. "I've been looking forward to meeting you in person."

His wife emerged from the kitchen moments later, wiping her hands on a dish towel. Wearing jeans and a loose shirt, her round face focused on Quincy. "Hi, I'm Dana. Logan said you need a safe haven for a bit, and that Delton wants to keep guard in your camper and give you the guest room. It sounds like a good plan to me. If you'll come to the kitchen with me, I'll pour you a cup of coffee that you can drink while I finish fixing supper."

"That sounds good," Quincy said, "but only if you'll let me help with the meal."

Dana grinned. "It's a deal. Come on."

As they left the room, Logan's green eyes fixed on Delton. "You like that gal, don't you?"

He shrugged. "Yeah. She seems like a good person."

Logan took a seat and indicated Delton do the same. "If you have more on your mind than just the case of her missing parents, I'm a good listener."

"There's nothing going on between us."

"But the potential is there."

He took the chair facing his friend and colleague. "Maybe. But her total focus right now is finding her parents."

"And you're focused on your missing persons cold case. But which is affecting you more, the case or the woman?"

Delton dragged in a deep breath. "They're both important to me."

Logan grinned. "That wasn't so bad to admit, was it?"

"She seems to put a lot of trust in God, and her adopted dad is a savvy journalist."

Logan visibly perked up at that. "I want to hear more details about this case and these people."

Chapter 7

Thursday's work shift passed in a blur for Quincy. Delton again rode the tram while she conducted tours. But no matter how busy she was, she couldn't shake the constant awareness she felt at his close presence.

"Erin called while you were making your last spiel." Delton kept pace beside her after she had parked the Jeep and headed to sign off duty. "She and Miles have finalized their wedding plans, so she and Ginger are returning to Springfield tomorrow and want us to join them and their fiancés for dinner at the steak house this evening. In fact, they ordered me to bring you. Are you okay with that?"

"They ordered you, huh?" She swung her head sideways, studying the quirk at the corners of his mouth. "Do you take orders well?"

"If it'll keep peace, I try." His tone was dry.

"What about your job? Are you off duty now?"

"I'm not on the clock, but I'm still your shadow. We may as well go enjoy a good meal."

She couldn't deny that it sounded good, especially when her stomach emitted a low growl. She flushed. "Let's go then."

When they entered the restaurant, they found the two

couples already sipping tea and coffee at a table in front of a large picture window with a clear view of the street.

"We're glad you came," Ginger said as they took the remaining two seats at the table.

"Are you all ready to order now?" a waitress asked, order pad in hand.

"Yes," Erin answered for the group.

Once their orders were placed, pleasant conversation ebbed and flowed until their meals arrived. After Jon offered a blessing, the meal claimed their attention, but Quincy couldn't escape her awareness of the detective seated next to her. Wearing casual attire of navy slacks and a light blue polo shirt, he was handsome to the point of breathtaking.

It wasn't until they were relaxing over desserts and coffee that the topic of conversation focused on Quincy.

"Will you tell us more about your search for your parents?" Ginger asked, eyeing her from across the table. "Do you think you were born here in Branson?"

Quincy drained her tea glass and set it down. "In this area," she qualified, nodding. "Growing up so close to where I was born makes me think someone here took me to that children's home in Springfield, and it wasn't a family member. It doesn't make a lot of sense."

"God must have protected you," Ginger theorized.

"It's clear that someone doesn't want her finding out how and why that happened," Delton said. "And we're going to do it. Does anyone here remember hearing anything about the Clayton or Ramsey couples back when they were performing at that theater?"

Silence fell as expressions turned thoughtful. After several moments Erin spoke. "When I was a kid growing up in Ozark, I remember a group of teenage boys used to hang out at a house up the street from us. I guess at least one of them must have been related to our neighbor. Anyhow, I was impressed that one of those boys was the son of people at a Branson theater. One day Sean Ramsey and another boy were fixing a flat tire, and Sean spoke to me in a friendly way as I rode past them on my bike. I was thrilled and mentioned it to my parents at supper that evening."

Quincy grinned, picturing the young girl enamored of an older boy. "Did they caution you about idolizing older boys?"

Erin returned the grin. "I'm sure they did. They also discussed the boy's parents later when they didn't know I was in the next room where I could hear them. Dad was talking about gambling in the area and told Mom he had heard that the Ramsey boy's dad was a heavy gambler. I don't know if that tidbit means anything or not, but your question brought it to mind."

Quincy frowned at Delton. "Did you know that?"

"No, I didn't. Maybe I need to talk to Sean again and see if I can find out more about the activities and reputation of his parents back then."

"When will you do that?"

He considered for a moment. "I need to do some research first."

"Is it possible I could run into Springfield to check on my dad?"

"You mean now?"

She nodded. "I have to work most weekends, like this coming one, so this is a good time. I try to go check on him as often as I can."

"Okay. We'll do that tonight, and I'll go to Rockaway Beach tomorrow."

"We'll go."

His brows rose. Then he heaved a sigh of capitulation. "Okay, we'll go."

"Thanks for inviting us," Quincy said to Erin and Ginger, gathering her purse. "I enjoyed it."

Five minutes later, they were on their way to Springfield. Seated beside him in his pickup, she let the silence reign for a few minutes before saying, "Thanks for doing this. Dad will probably grill us, but he's a good sounding board if you want to take advantage of him."

"I might do that," he said, not taking his gaze off the highway.

By the time they reached the edge of Springfield, the gray of dark was cloaking the landscape. As the sun sank below the tree lines, the sky glowed with orange and yellow streaks.

Wanting to know more about Delton, Quincy took advantage of having him a captive audience. "Are you from here originally?"

"Yeah," he said, offering no further information. But she noticed his stiff posture and tight grip on the steering wheel—and decided she should drop the subject.

"Are you sorry you started your ancestry search?" he asked.

"No. Something bad apparently happened to my parents, and I think the truth, whatever it is, needs to be revealed. God will protect me."

"I'll help Him," he said, rather than downplaying her assertion.

Moments later, he exited the interstate and followed her directions to the section of the city where Gary lived. When he had parked in front of the house, they crossed the yard together and mounted the front steps. Delton knocked on the door and stepped back.

When Gary opened the door and saw them, he looked up from his wheelchair and grabbed Quincy's hand. He tugged her down to him. "Get in here and tell me the details about all that's been happening to you."

She returned his embrace, came erect, and shot Delton an I-warned-you glance.

"You, too," Gary said to Delton, hand gesturing for him to enter as he whirled the chair around. "I want to thank you for looking out for my girl."

~

Delton overlooked the man's slightly imperious manner, understanding his concern for his daughter, which he considered indicative of a caring parent.

"If you want anything to eat or drink, Quincy knows where to find it." Gary pointed toward the kitchen.

"I don't need anything. We just ate," Quincy said, dropping onto the sofa.

"Same here." Delton sat beside her.

Quincy drew a deep breath and brought Gary up to date.

"You need to come home," he declared when she finished. "I never should have encouraged you in this search. I can't risk losing you." He rubbed a hand across his eyes.

Delton leaned forward, sympathizing with the man. "She needs to see it through. Whatever secrets have come to life aren't going to go away. They have to be dealt with so the threats against her will end."

Gary beamed a long, intense stare at him. Then he exhaled sharply. "I guess you're right, but I don't have to like it. Will you promise to keep her safe?"

"I'll do my best. There's another detail I forgot to tell you."

Gary leaned forward. "Tell me."

"Your daughter and I visited the Recorder of Deeds office and learned that the Country Cuzzins Theater was sold to the current owner by Mr. and Mrs. Ramsey, but the deed is a forgery."

Gary's head did a slow bob of understanding. "So there's real estate theft involved. That convinces me more than ever that the Claytons aren't alive. And whoever killed them wants Quincy gone, too, so she can't expose them."

"I can't let them get away with it," Quincy declared, her fists clenched. "If my parents were killed, they deserve justice."

Delton focused on Gary. "Will you tell me about Quincy's adoption again?"

Gary gripped the arms of his chair tightly, visibly

clamping down on his emotions. "Sarah and I had given up on having children of our own and began seeking a child to adopt. When the children's home called and said they had a little girl we could possibly adopt, we were ecstatic and raced right over there. And fell in love with Quincy on sight."

"Were you given any background on her?"

"Only that her name was Quincy. The nurse said they found her in the foyer early one morning, sitting in an infant seat. A note was found underneath the cushion. All it said was 'Her name is Quincy. She's fourteen months old.'"

"That's all?"

Gary nodded. "They talked to the police, and there were never any missing child reports of a baby by that name and age, so they eventually made her available for adoption, wanting her to have a good home."

"I had that," Quincy assured him, reaching over and squeezing his hand. "And I thank you."

He blinked back tears. "We loved you. Now go find out what happened to the people God used to bring you into this world."

They chatted a few more minutes and left.

"Are you planning to go to work with me tomorrow?" Quincy asked once they were back on the interstate.

"Yep." He darted a look over at her and saw her mouth and brows scrunch into a frown.

"You don't need to do that. I'll be safe at work. And you have other cases at your job."

He wrestled the matter for several moments. He hated to leave her, but he needed to clear up some paperwork at the office. "How about we compromise? I'll talk to the security guard in the morning. If he can keep a close eye on you, I'll go to my office, and you can call me any time."

He reached over and pressed a finger against her lips, and the action inadvertently sent goose bumps crawling up his arm. "I'll relieve the guard at lunch time and spend the afternoon with you."

"Okay," she relented, "but that doesn't mean I like being babied."

~

After another night at the Fuller home, Quincy was glad to go to work, even if Delton did insist on taking her. Logan and his family were pleasant and seemed to truly want her with them, but she didn't want to interfere with their routines.

"I'll bring a pizza for lunch," Delton said when he dropped her off at the tram where the security guard was waiting to meet them.

She wrinkled her nose at him. "That might improve my mood."

He chuckled. "See you."

After an uneventful day, Quincy signed off duty and climbed wearily into the passenger seat of Delton's unmarked police car, hoping to relax and decompress during the few miles drive to Rockaway Beach.

He glanced over at her as he started the engine. "Do you need to work during the summer?"

"I just thought it was a way to integrate into the community and help me get to know people who would answer questions. But I admit I may have made a mistake."

"Why don't you quit then?"

"I hate to leave them shorthanded with the tourist season in full swing."

"I'm sure they handle a certain amount of turnover every season."

"I know. But I hate to break a commitment." She sat up straighter as another thought hit her. "Do you think my presence is a danger to others?"

"I'm afraid it could be. That first attack was at work," he reminded her. "So was the shooting."

She heaved a sigh. "Maybe you're right."

"Give it some thought, but be prepared to bail in a hurry

if there's another attack on you." He exited Highway 65 toward Rockaway Beach. Minutes later, he parked in front of the building where Sean Ramsey lived. They went to his apartment, and Delton rang the bell. After another ring, he faced Quincy. "I guess he's not home."

They turned and headed back to the exit—and met the desk clerk coming through the doorway.

"You wouldn't know where we could find Mr. Ramsey, your tenant in room 218, would you?" Delton asked him.

The middle-aged man frowned. "No, but if I were looking for him, I'd check the bar down the street."

"Thanks. We'll do that."

They exited the building and scanned the area. "I see it." Delton pointed toward a building at the end of the block on the other side of the street.

They crossed the street, walked down the sidewalk, and entered the bar. The big roughly finished room was smoky and dimly lit, but Quincy spotted Sean at a table near the far wall. She tipped her head in that direction. "Over there."

They crossed the room and took seats across from him. "We'd like to talk to you some more," Delton said, his tone making it mandatory.

They were met with a glare that spoke volumes. "I already talked to you," Sean growled, his tone bordering on hostility.

"But you didn't tell us as much as you could have," Quincy blurted, fighting the urge to ask outright if he knew where her parents were.

"I don't know any more," he snapped, picking up the bottle near his hand and swigging from it, his eyes closed as if that would make them go away.

"We're not here to cause you trouble," Delton said. "We know you were just a teenager at the time of interest to us. But you were old enough to see and hear things going on around you."

Sean peered at him through bleary eyes, wary caution in

them. Then his expression slowly softened a little. "I hung around the theater and did some odd jobs."

"So you knew your parents' partners and the people who worked for them."

He shrugged. "Yeah."

"Did you know your dad liked to gamble?"

Another shrug. "He played poker with his buddies. So what?"

"He apparently didn't want us to talk to your mother, so he gave us an old address. Will you give us her current one?"

Sean sat in stony silence for several moments. Then he seemed to deflate. "She and Ben are in the Wilshire Apartments." He quoted the room number.

"Thanks. You do remember the Claytons, don't you?"

"Yeah," he muttered sullenly, "but I didn't see much of them. I mostly did odd jobs when the theater was empty except for workers or hung out in the lobby and ate popcorn with Trixie."

Quincy's interest piqued. "Who's Trixie?"

"A girl close to my age whose mom worked as a maid at the theater."

"What's her last name?"

He spread his hands, palms up. "I don't know. She was Trixie Scranton back then. It could be anything now."

"What was her mother's name?" Delton asked, making notes.

Sean's frown deepened. He scanned the ceiling in thoughtful mode. Then he shook his head. "I just called her Mrs. Scranton. I don't remember a first name."

Delton pushed to his feet. "Thanks for leveling with us."

Once they were hoofing it back to his car, Quincy spoke. "He was a kid when my parents disappeared. You surely don't think he killed them."

"No, but I still think he knows more than he's admitting. And his life seems to have gone off track around that time."

They arrived at the car, climbed inside, and headed back

to Branson. "What are you going to do now?" she asked.

"I'm going to look for that girl and her mother. They might remember something vital. Every trail has to be followed. Are you hungry?"

"A little," she admitted. "And I don't want your friend to have to feed us."

They stopped at a restaurant and ate quickly. Though outwardly calm, Quincy's insides fluttered at their closeness as they returned to the car. Delton's broad shoulders and six foot height made her feel small beside him.

At the passenger door, he reached past her to open it, and she caught his warm, strictly masculine scent. She licked at suddenly dry lips.

He was close enough to touch. The urge to press her hand against his chest, feel his heartbeat under the fabric of his shirt, shook her.

She gazed into his eyes. When she saw his pupils darken, she knew he felt it, too—a strange and exciting bond between them.

He closed his eyes, and the connection was broken.

Was she insane?

Sanity returning in full force, she practically plunged inside the vehicle.

Chapter 8

"**Her name is** now Trixie Albertson," Delton said as he put the car in motion. Quincy had just gotten off work Saturday, and they were going to see the woman. "She lives a few miles out of town, but works at one of the local theaters."

Quincy settled back in the seat. "Is she the same age as Sean Ramsey?"

"She's a year older. He's forty, and she's forty-one. I considered calling her, but decided an unexpected visit might be more productive, not give her time to decide what to tell and what to keep to herself. I checked her work schedule at the theater, and she's off today, so hopefully we'll catch her at home."

"You've been busy," she commented, studying the horizon where the sky was a soft cloudless blue. It was still a beautiful day. He sensed that she loved the peace and beauty of these rolling hills and green countryside as much as he did.

After a period of quiet, she looked his way. "What kind of trouble does the forged deed mean for that theater owner?"

"I'm sure Mr. Carruthers is worried. He needs to consult

with a real estate attorney, which I'm sure he has. They'll need to locate the notary whose name is on the deed—if he's still around after all this time. They'll also have a title search done. The fraudsters have to be caught and charges filed against them."

"What about a handwriting expert? Will they need one?"

"Likely. It'll probably be a mess to wade through." Following GPS directions, he activated his turn signal and eased off the highway. Miles later, he arrived at Trixie's house and pulled into the driveway that was lined on each side by flower bushes. The yard was neat, the grass recently mowed.

He parked, and they headed across the lawn to the house. As they reached the porch steps, a woman came around the corner of the building. She looked the right age, her brown hair in a ponytail and wearing khaki shorts and a white tank top that bore signs of working in the yard or garden. Carrying a pair of pruning shears, she came to an abrupt halt.

Delton approached her. "Are you Trixie Albertson?"

Her face tightened, her gaze darting to Quincy. "Yes," she said in a slow drawl.

"I'm Detective Delton Booker."

"And I'm Quincy Clark," Quincy cut in, edging near and extending a hand.

The woman's eyes rounded, and Delton thought her face went a shade lighter. "I have some questions I'd like to ask you. Do you remember Sean Ramsey?"

Her thin lips formed a frown. "Yes, I remember him. Why?"

"Do you remember his parents and their partners?"

She shrugged, her eyes darting a glance at Quincy. "I saw them around. They owned a theater and did a show there. But I had almost no acquaintance beyond that."

"Sean said your mother worked at that theater."

"That's right. She was a maid there." She glanced at her watch, her manner striking him as nervous.

"Do you remember when the partners ended their relationship?"

She shook her head slowly. "I was just a teenager then and more interested in boys than anything the adults were doing. Then the Claytons were gone. Sean said they ended the partnership and moved away. When the theater was sold months later, my mom went to work at another theater. I work at that one now, but Mom's retired."

"Those partners were my parents," Quincy said. "And they've not been seen or heard from in the twenty-five years since then. Did you ever hear any talk about where they went?"

Delton thought the woman flushed a little. He wasn't sure what to make of it.

"No. Or if I did, I don't remember it," Trixie said. "My only interest was Sean. But he started seeing a girl who was in his own class around that time."

"So, you and Sean never dated?"

"Like I said, he started dating someone else. Even though he was a year behind me in school, I had a crush on him, so I stopped hanging around where I could see them together. Later, I started dating Brandon. We married right after graduation. And he's due home from work any time now."

They thanked her for her time and left.

"She and Sean may have been young, but they weren't little kids," he said when they were back inside the car.

"And they both know more than they're telling," Quincy finished the thought. "Are you going to talk to the mother?"

Delton stared straight ahead while driving. "You bet, I am. And hopefully before Trixie has time to contact her. Because of her known work history, I found her address before Trixie's."

If they kept finding and questioning people, surely

someone would provide a tidbit of information that would steer them to Quincy's parents—or what had happened to them.

~

"Is there nothing else you remember about that time?" Quincy asked, frustrated at the lack of information obtained. Mrs. Scranton was an older version of her daughter, the same eyes and features, but the hair was streaked with gray and white. The living room where they sat had gray carpet that was threadbare but clean—as were the furnishings.

The woman had answered Delton's questions in what seemed a forthright manner to Quincy. "I always figured something must have scared the Claytons into bailing out of the business and leaving so fast. I couldn't believe it when I heard they were gone," she said, shaking her head.

"What could have happened that would have scared them enough to leave town so suddenly?" Delton asked, leaning forward on the cushion of the blue and white striped sofa where he sat beside Quincy. "Was there anything going on that could have been troublesome, problems between the partners maybe?"

"I never thought anything was scary. And the two couples seemed to get along well."

Quincy watched the play of expression on the woman's face. Her face crinkled in thought, she sat for several moments, and then a hand went to her chin and rubbed it, as if unable to say whatever was bothering her.

Quincy scooted off the sofa, knelt before the woman, and seized the hand that lay on the arm of the rocker. "The Claytons were my parents, and I need to find out what happened to them. If you know anything, anything at all, that could help us do that, won't you please tell us?"

Slowly the woman turned her gaze onto Quincy for several moments. Then she drew a deep breath and opened her tightly pressed lips. "I'm not sure, but I think there was something going on at the theater after the night shows ended and the employees left. I worked the earlier shifts," she added, her voice having developed a slight quaver.

"Do you know what it was?" Delton asked.

"I never asked," she replied hesitantly. "I guess I didn't want to know. But when I happened to drive by there to pick up my daughter from a late activity, I would see quite a few cars in the parking lot."

"What did you suspect was happening that late?"

"I'm not sure," she said slowly, "but I wondered if a bunch of friends were meeting there for poker games."

"Why did you think it was poker?"

"Because I recognized the fancy car of a man I had heard was a heavy gambler. And the other vehicles were the expensive kind that people who have lots of money tend to drive."

"Can you give me the name of the person you heard was a heavy gambler?" Delton asked.

"I don't want to cause trouble for anyone," she said, frowning.

"That will only happen if evidence of criminal activity is found," he assured her.

"And he won't know where you got his name if you find anything?"

"I'll do my best to keep your name out of it."

She drew a deep breath. "It was Burnell Romano."

Delton made a note.

"Thank you, Mrs. Scranton," Quincy said, squeezing her hand and releasing it. She stood and looked at Delton.

He gave her a head nod that signaled it was time to leave.

As they returned to the car, Quincy grinned at Delton. "The Romano name sounds like a mobster."

~

Delton grinned back at her. "You might be right. I plan to do some thorough research on him. This woman didn't strike me as secretive like her daughter and Sean." He eyed the dimple at her mouth. Funny he hadn't noticed that before now. In the bright sunlight her dark hair gleamed. He squelched the sudden and unusual urge to touch it.

"Time to roll," he said, opening the car door. He had a decent life, was happy—most of the time. He needed to be alone, sort out the feelings eating at him.

Delton attended church with Quincy Sunday morning, reminding himself it was to guard her. But he couldn't keep his gaze from trailing to her face regularly.

He struggled to keep his focus on the sermon, but found it alarming when the pastor spoke of John writing to the church of Laodicea and reprimanding them for being neither hot nor cold.

"Cold water is good for drinking," Pastor Richardson stated. "Hot springs have healing qualities. A lukewarm person is one who has lost his dependence on God. Let's don't be that way, but be passionate about loving and depending on God and sharing with others about Him."

When the service was over, Delton pushed guilt aside and accompanied Quincy outside. But the warmth of the service comforted him.

As they walked to the parking lot, his phone rang. It was Logan. He answered, listened to what he had to say, and ended the call.

"He's been doing more research on Allen Ramsey's ex," he related to Quincy. "He says the guy she married is a partner in a new theater, and she works there. Not all the theaters do shows on Sunday, but this one does. It starts at two."

"So that's where we're going."

He nodded. "After we eat."

An hour later, they drove to the theater, and Delton asked the woman at the gift counter if they could speak to Sharleen Bledsoe. Her frown of reluctance morphed to one of compliance when he showed his badge. She beckoned for them to follow her down a hallway. She stopped at a doorway and knocked.

"Come in," a muffled voice sounded from inside.

The woman opened the door and motioned for them to enter. She left as they stepped inside the room.

The woman behind the desk looked up, her gaze raking over them in sharp assessment.

Delton flashed his badge again. "I'm Detective Booker, and I need to ask you some questions." He motioned Quincy to a chair and took the one beside it.

Sharleen Bledsoe stood, her lips in a thin line, her stance authoritative. "What is this about? We have a show to do in less than an hour."

"Then let's get at it," Delton said briskly. "We're working on a cold case and looking for the Clayton couple who disappeared years ago—your former partners."

She gripped the edge of the desk and sank back into her chair. "I thought they just moved out of state. Why are you looking for them after all this time?"

The arrogance he had noted in her had abated somewhat. Delton saw the speculative glances she darted at Quincy. The woman was wired tight enough to shoot off of that seat at the least trigger.

"This is Quincy Clark. The Claytons were her parents, and she's looking for them."

Sharleen frowned. "Quincy?" She leaned forward on the desk, studying her.

Quincy nodded, but remained seated. "Yes. I was left at a children's home when I was a baby. Weeks later, a couple took me as a foster child and adopted me after the home had cleared the hurdles for that to be possible."

"When is the last time you saw the Claytons?" Delton asked, hoping shock would shake her enough to give up whatever she knew.

Sharleen's head rotated back and forth. "I thought they took you with them."

"My DNA says they didn't." Quincy's tone was flat.

Sharleen eased back and shifted in the chair. Her expression turned icy. "So what do you want from me? I haven't seen them since they bailed out of the business and walked out the door."

"I want you to tell me why they left."

Her expression turned frosty. "They said they were tired of the business and wanted out."

"Did you buy their share of the theater?"

"We did. And it wasn't easy to come up with that much money so fast."

Delton figured that confirmed her complicity in the forged deed. "Do you think there were more reasons for their sudden departure than just being tired of the business?"

She frowned. "I didn't at the time, but I've wondered since if they were running away from something."

"Was illegal gambling taking place in the theater?"

She drew up short, her gaze startled—and stony. Then she shook her head. "Of course not." She hesitated. "But now that you mention it, they were in a terrible hurry to leave. So maybe there was something going on that we didn't know about."

"Did you know Burnell Romano?"

She shrugged, a flash of annoyance crossing that artfully made up face. "I knew the name. That's all. Why? Is he someone who could have been giving them trouble?"

She was cagey. Delton gave her that. His gut said she knew—or had known—the man well.

She glanced at her watch, a direct signal that her time was valuable. "I need to go."

As she rounded the desk, clearly leaving, Delton and Quincy both stood. At the door, Sharleen opened it for them to exit.

Delton paused in front of her. "I'm going to find out what happened to your former partners. If you think of anything that could be helpful, give me a call." He handed her his card.

He and Quincy didn't speak until they were back inside his vehicle. Then she swiveled in the seat to face him. "What did you make of that?"

Delton exhaled deeply and shook his head. "She knows something. And I think your appearance shook her. Or she's a very good actress."

"Well, she is in show business," Quincy said sardonically. "So what next?"

"We'll give her some time to stew over our visit. Then, if we haven't made enough progress, we'll come back and rattle her cage."

Chapter 9

Quincy wasn't thrilled about going to work the next morning, but she couldn't just quit without notice. Fortunately, the job kept her busy enough to hold her tangled thoughts at bay.

When her first load of tourists filled the tram after lunch, an attractive woman who appeared to be in her fifties cast a searching look over Quincy as she boarded. Slender and well groomed, a few wrinkles surrounded her hazel eyes. She took a seat at the front of the tram and eased back. Throughout the tour Quincy sensed the woman's watchful gaze behind her, giving her the impression more than once during stops at landmarks that she wanted to speak to her. But there was never an opportunity to do that.

It made her uneasy when the woman boarded again for the last tour of the day. This time she sat further back in the tram and kept her distance. Quincy parked at the end of the tour and left the Jeep to stand at the front of the tram and watch the tourists disembark. When the woman remained seated until she was the last person to exit, Quincy welcomed the sight of Delton stepping from his seat to confront her.

"Is there something bothering you, Ma'am?" he asked, his tone firm, but not harsh.

The woman nodded, licking her lips nervously. "I'd like to speak to the driver if she has time." Her gaze darted to Quincy.

Quincy motioned her to sit on the front seat. "What would you like to talk about?"

"Well," she said slowly, sinking onto the seat, "I heard about a shooting here at the parking lot, and then I …I heard your name and …and that you're looking for your parents." A hand went over her mouth, her eyes glistening and blinking.

Quincy darted a quick look up at Delton's protective stance, signaling that this was no threat. Then she sat next to the woman and spoke softly. "Tell me who you are and why you've come looking for me. Does it have anything to do with my parents?"

The woman nodded in short jerks. "I'm Holly Lindstrom. Janet Clayton was my friend. I loved her baby Quincy. Are you sure you're that child?"

"I've had DNA matches to some relatives of Janet and Drake Clayton that say I am."

The tears flowed freely now. "I have something, too." She pulled her purse from her side and opened it. Then she pulled out a picture and handed it to Quincy. "That's you as a baby."

Delton scooted onto the seat behind them and peered over Quincy's shoulder. "She was a cute little thing."

His masculine scent made Quincy's stomach flutter. She forced her eyes to stay focused on the picture.

Holly extracted another picture and placed it beside the infant's image. "I took it to a lab technician and had him use his facial recognition technology to create a simulated image of what you might look like as an adult. It's how I recognized you."

Delton chuckled. "It's a close resemblance."

Quincy stared at the picture, amazed at the likeness to her, and touched to the core that this woman had cared enough about her mother to search so hard for her. "Thank you so much for doing this," she said past the constriction in her throat and putting her arms around the woman.

When she pulled back, she sniffed and swiped at her eyes. "You must have been close to my mother to do this."

Holly nodded. "I was. We spent a lot of time together. I grew up in this town and met Janet in church choir when we were both about twenty. We became instant friends. I even sang with them a few times in their show."

"So you knew their partners as well," Delton said, shifting to the seat across the aisle facing them and leaning forward, his hands on his knees.

She nodded, her expression solemn. "The two couples performed well together on stage. I never spent much personal time around the Ramseys, so I didn't know them the way I did the Claytons."

"Did the two couples get along well?"

"So far as I know. I never heard them argue or anything like that. But ..." She paused, taking on an air of remembrance. "I once overheard the Ramsey couple in a heated argument," she continued after several moments.

"Do you know what it was about?" Quincy asked before Delton could.

Holly frowned. "I can't remember details, but it seems in my mind that something was yelled that sounded like one of them, I'm not sure which, might have been ...well, involved with someone else. It was after a show, and the theater had emptied. I had been chatting with Janet and was late leaving," she explained in a rush. "As I walked past an office with the door slightly open, I heard their voices."

So there could have been marital problems. And they did end up divorced. But that wouldn't have anything to do with my parents dropping out of sight. Quincy pushed the thoughts aside.

"A couple of days later I tried to call Janet and couldn't get an answer," Holly continued. "I never saw or heard from her again. I went to the theater and asked the Ramseys about her. They said the Claytons had sold out and left them, and they didn't know where they had gone. I went to their house and found it empty. I've always felt that something bad happened to them, but I can't imagine what. I've wondered over the years if they could have driven into a lake or something like that. All I know in my heart is that they wouldn't have just up and disappeared like that without letting me, or someone, know—and never returning."

Quincy gave her another quick hug.

"And now that you've turned up looking for them and been attacked, I'm more certain than ever that something bad happened," she added, choking on the words.

"I have one more question," Delton said gently. "Do you know if there was anything besides music shows going on at that theater?"

Holly's eyes went wide, her body still. "They rented the basement to someone," she said after an awkward pause. "I'm not sure about the details."

"Could gambling have been going on down there?"

She closed her eyes for several seconds and reopened them. "I didn't believe it, but one time I heard someone say they thought there was a casino hidden down there," she admitted in a near whisper. "My husband thought it was true. I didn't want to believe it. It worried me."

"Does the name Burnell Romano mean anything to you?"

She frowned, deep in thought. "It sounds familiar, but I can't place it," she said moments later. "I'm sorry. That's all I know."

"Can we keep in touch?" Quincy asked, embracing her again. "I'd like to hear about my mother. My adopted one died of cancer," she explained, drawing back and pulling a pen and notepad from her purse. She jotted her phone number on it and handed it to Holly.

Holly smiled, her mouth and chin trembling. "I'd love

that."

After putting the note in her purse, she left them, but turned back and waved multiple times as she walked away.

"We have to talk to Mr. Ramsey in more depth," Delton said, coming to his feet and tugging Quincy up beside him.

"You bet, we do," she agreed. "He knows what happened to my parents, or has information that can lead to finding them."

~

Within minutes of Quincy signing off duty, Delton drove them to Allen Ramsey's home in Fayetteville and parked. He wished he didn't have Quincy with him, but he knew she wanted to face the man again. And he didn't want her out of his sight.

They hiked to the door in the waning daylight, and he rang the doorbell loud and long.

It suddenly flew open. "What are you doing back here?" their quarry demanded angrily, his ruddy face reddening further.

"We came to have another chat," Delton said, squelching the urge to punch the snarl off the man's face.

"You can't harass people like this."

"I'm not harassing you. I'm just dropping by to give you an opportunity to clear up some contradictions in that first chat we had."

"I don't have to talk to you." Resentment billowed from him.

"You can talk to me, or come to the police station and talk to the chief. It's your choice. Your *only* choice."

The man hesitated in the act of slamming the door. He glowered in angry defiance for several long moments.

"Your partners went missing, and you never talked to the police about it."

"Being missing isn't a crime," he shot back.

"Why did you lie about buying out their interest in the theater?" Delton asked, accepting that they would not be invited inside.

"I didn't," he denied angrily.

"You did. Clayton's signature on the theater deed was forged. What did you do to your partners?"

"Nothing!" he shouted. Then some of the fight seemed to drain out of him.

"But that deed was forged. Why?"

Ramsey glanced around, as if seeking inspiration. Then he stiffened his back and hissed, "Okay, it was forged."

"I know that, but thank you for confirming it. I assume you know it's a criminal offense," he threw in pointedly before continuing with a bluff. "We also know that you were running a hidden casino in the basement."

"I wasn't," he denied hotly.

"Somebody was," Delton persisted. "Was it you and your partners? Or was Burnell Romano also a partner in it?"

"The Claytons and Romano were doing it. Something went wrong between them, and the Claytons got out of Dodge, leaving me holding the bag. I had to sell the place to get out of debt and pay off Romano."

Delton didn't buy the story. "The guy who bought the theater from you knows the deed was forged, and I'm sure he's preparing to press charges. You can go talk to my police chief, or I can take you there. It's your choice."

Caught—and mad as a raging bull—Ramsey closed the door and stalked to his car.

After following the man to the station and escorting him to the chief's office, Delton was relieved at being told to go home and keep Quincy under close watch. Chief Crenshaw would talk to him tomorrow.

After driving to the Fullers and seeing Quincy inside, he went to the den where he had left his laptop and logged onto a search site. He was able to find that, although Romano was suspected in a string of gambling related incidents and assaults, he was never prosecuted until a few years ago. He had been convicted and gone to prison.

Logan entered the room before he could find any more information. He eyed the laptop. "Come to supper before Dana throws it out. Let's discuss the case after we eat."

~

Quincy was already seated at the table with Dana and the two kids when Logan and Delton entered the kitchen. Logan offered a blessing, and they focused on the meal.

Afterward, the kids went to their rooms, and the adults cleaned the kitchen and migrated to the living room with cups of coffee. Quincy had told Delton she wanted to move back into her camper or stay at the hotel, but his friends had insisted they wanted her to stay with them until certain of her safety and had gone out of their way to put her at ease.

"Have you made any progress on finding Quincy's parents?" Dana asked Delton. A petite blond, her hair was long and straight. She seemed intelligent and worked at a bank downtown.

"We talked to a woman who worked at that theater back when the Claytons were there," Delton explained. "She mentioned seeing people there after show hours and provided the name of a man she remembers seeing as Burnell Romano, a known gambler, among them. Then we got Allen Ramsey to admit that there was a casino in the basement, with Romano involved. The man is well known to law enforcement and went to prison years ago."

The idea that her parents could have been involved in such an operation shook Quincy. She couldn't accept the idea.

"I'll be back," Logan said. "I'm going to dig around and see if I can find anything to indicate there was such an operation going on under everyone's noses."

Quincy mentally thumped her head, confused. "Why would they do such a thing—if they did?"

"Money," Dana supplied promptly. "And when big money is involved, other things tend to go along with it."

"Like what?" Quincy asked.

Dana shrugged. "A number of things come to mind. Illegal casino owners tend to branch out into operations like loan sharking, extortion, drugs, counterfeiting, money laundering, porn and prostitution."

She worked in a bank, so Quincy figured she had extensive knowledge of such schemes. She closed her eyes, shuddering at the scope of possibilities. Then she opened them and took a deep breath. "I refuse to believe my parents were doing any of those things until I've seen absolute proof. But I need to know the truth, no matter what it is. We have to talk to that Burnell Romano and make him tell us if he killed them."

"He sounds like the kind of guy who could have done it," Logan announced, reentering the room. "But he won't be confessing." He dropped onto an overstuffed chair near the fireplace.

"Where is he?"

He grimaced. "In a cemetery somewhere. He was convicted of manslaughter several years after your parents disappeared. But he got out of prison two years ago and was killed days later by a thug he had double-crossed in a deal."

Quincy sank back onto the sofa cushion. "Then we'll never know if the Claytons were among his victims."

Two young bodies came hurtling into the room. "Momma, Jerry won't let me have the remote," the four-year-old girl wailed.

"She took it from me," the six-year-old boy said, clearly on the verge of snatching it.

Dana stood, a hand extended. "Give it to me. And you two take your baths, brush your teeth, and get ready for bed."

Quincy grinned as the children were ushered back out of the room.

"They're tired and cranky," Logan said with a sigh. "But Dana's good with them. She'll have them back in good spirits soon."

"I think I'd better call it a day," Delton said, grinning

and rising from the sofa.

Quincy stood also. To her surprise, he escorted her up the hallway to the guest room. He paused at the doorway and placed his hands on her shoulders to turn her toward him. "Don't be discouraged," he said softly.

"But we may never find out what happened." She couldn't prevent the despair she felt from coloring her tone.

A soft light gleamed from his eyes. "We're not giving up."

"What do you plan to do?"

"Catch up with Mr. Ramsey's ex-wife again and see how closely their stories match. Then I may need to talk to the man again."

She nodded. "Thank you for helping me. Yes, I know it's your job," she added quickly when he started to speak. "But I feel like you've been a friend to me, understood my motives. That has meant a lot to me."

"I guess I needed a friend, too," he said, a hand reaching out to brush a strand of hair away from her cheek. The depths of his gaze made her knees turn to gelatin.

When he leaned over and pressed a kiss against her temple, all rational thought left her mind. And when he kissed her lips, the breath left her body.

After a brief, wonderful moment, he pulled back. Then he spun on his heel and strode down the hallway.

Chapter 10

Tuesday morning, Delton sat facing Chief Crenshaw across his desk. Having left Quincy in the care of the security guard at the Homestead, he had brought his boss up to date on meeting Holly Lindstrom, as well as the second visit with Allen Ramsey.

He leaned back in the chair, hoping the chief couldn't read his frustration. "I may need to talk to that theater owner some more about his deed, but I want to pick up the warrant we requested and go to the bank."

"I'll see that the deed issue is handled. You keep after new leads and let us deal with details."

With that promise, Delton left the office. Thirty minutes later he had a warrant in hand and headed across town. He pulled in at the bank and parked in the lot. Inside the modern brick structure, he approached the nearest of the four desks in the lobby. "I'd like to speak to the manager," he said to the woman seated there, showing his badge.

She pushed an intercom button. "There's a police officer here asking to see you." She paused. "Okay."

She shifted her attention back to Delton. "Mr. Dunham's office is the one at the end of the hall on the left." She pointed across the lobby.

Delton went to it and opened the door. The suit clad man behind the desk looked up from his computer, stood, and extended a hand across the desk. "Good morning, Officer. I'm Joseph Dunham. How may I help you?"

"I need to see the financial records of any accounts and safety deposit box Drake and Janet Clayton had with you." He shook the hand and placed the warrant on the desk.

The manager frowned, shaking his head. "I don't recall the name."

"They disappeared over twenty years ago."

His expression cleared. "Yes, I have it now. This must be related to that news story about the daughter searching for them and being attacked."

"That's right."

"I can already tell you about it, but let me pull up the information here. Just have a seat." He turned to his computer and began tapping keys.

Delton didn't have to wait long.

"Here we go. I'll print this for you." He started the print process and faced Delton again. "Banks are required to turn over funds and property from an inactive account to the unclaimed-property office of state treasury, as was done in this case. Once the account is sent to the state in a process called escheating, the funds and contents of the box are held as unclaimed property. The couple had a joint personal account with a balance of just over five thousand dollars. There's a list there of the box contents on the second printout."

Delton accepted the papers the man handed him. He quickly read over the list that included a few pieces of jewelry, two car titles, and a life insurance policy with a familiar company. "Thank you, Sir. You've been very helpful."

Once inside his vehicle, he pulled out his cell phone and called that insurance company.

"The cash value of that policy was depleted paying the

premiums years ago," the agent he reached informed him after checking their records. "Is there anything else I can do for you?"

Delton thanked the woman and disconnected. Now he would resume the task of guarding Quincy for the rest of the day, a thought that brought an acceleration of his heart rate— which was insane. How many times did he have to be reminded that he had no business being attracted to someone involved in a police case? He didn't want or need the distraction.

Yet questions plagued him. Had she always been single? Was she divorced? Dealing with a broken relationship? Possibly widowed?

He shook his head to clear it and started the engine. Minutes later he pulled into the Homestead parking lot.

~

Quincy had climbed off the Jeep to take her lunch break when she spotted Delton's pickup pulling into the parking lot. She appreciated him driving his personal vehicle and wearing civilian clothes when riding the tram.

"It looks like my relief has arrived," the security guard said. "See you next time I'm needed. Stay safe." He strode away.

When Delton started walking toward her, Quincy saw that he carried a fast food bag. "Let's eat outside," she said, waving at the table near the edge of the lot where employees sat to eat and visit in clear weather. "And next time we do this, I buy."

He shrugged. "It's no big deal, just burgers and sodas."

"Coke for me and Root Beer for you?"

He grinned. "Yep."

They had just scooted onto the bench seat when Quincy's phone rang. "It's my dad," she said to him before answering. "What's up, Big Daddy?"

Gary's snort entered her ear. "Don't be smart with me, my girl. It sounds like you're okay. Tell me what progress you've made."

She gave him a quick overview, trying to ignore the burger in front of her. "What are you doing?" she asked, knowing he couldn't keep from poking around in the case.

"Nothing," he denied, too easily. "But there's something I'd like to do. Could you come back here for supper and then take me to visit your Aunt Jocelyn? I'd like to meet her."

He asked so little of her, and gave so much, she couldn't deny him outright. "Just a minute." She covered the phone with her hand and faced Delton.

He put his drink down. "What?"

"Could we go have supper with Dad this evening and then visit Aunt Jocelyn with him?"

He considered for a few moments. "I'll be off duty then, and a free meal sounds good. We can leave as soon as you get off work."

She returned the phone to her ear. "Look for us about six."

The busy afternoon passed quickly, and they headed toward Springfield as soon as they had signed off duty from their respective jobs. Quincy missed her van, but accepted that Delton's pickup would blend into traffic and be less identifiable.

She had mixed feelings about him hauling her around like this. She enjoyed his company—too much—but hated the circumstances that made it necessary.

"Are you okay?"

Delton's soft query jerked her from her muddled introspection.

"Yeah, I'm fine. I just wish we could find the answers to my parents' whereabouts—and who's trying to keep me from finding them."

"We will."

Comfortable silence reigned for the remainder of the drive. When they reached the edge of town, he followed the remembered route to her dad's house.

"You said you don't live here, didn't you?" Delton asked as he parked in the driveway.

She shook her head. "I have my own apartment about a mile away. Dad wants his independence, and …"

"So do you," he finished for her, grinning. "I get it. My house is several miles from my mom, but I drop in on her once or twice a week."

She hadn't thought much about his personal life, but now she was curious. "Do you have siblings?"

"My sister, who's a couple of years younger than me, is married and lives in Little Rock." He opened the driver's door, slid to the ground, and came around to meet her.

Before they could ring the doorbell, the door swung open to reveal Gary facing them from his wheelchair. "Food's on the table. Come in and eat before it gets cold, and I throw it out." He extended a hand to Delton.

After a handshake, he eased back in his chair. "Follow me." He beckoned.

As they entered the house, the smell of Italian seasoning drifted from the kitchen. "Is it spaghetti or lasagna?" Quincy asked.

"It's lasagna, because I know you like it best."

She smirked at his back and grinned over at Delton. "He thinks he's paying me for coming."

"I heard that," Gary called back at her.

"If this is your idea of payment, I might forget to go home," she warned.

"That's fine." Gary spun the chair around and looked at Delton. "You can pour the iced tea when Quincy gets ice in the glasses."

Delton smiled. "I can do that."

Moments later, Gary said a blessing and they dug into the meal. He pushed the platter of garlic bread toward Delton. "We need to take my van to the nursing home because it's modified for me." He was a take charge person.

Conversation flowed on light topics, but Quincy knew that wouldn't be the case the entire evening. Her situation was bound to be discussed at the nursing home, if not sooner.

They ate quickly and chased the food with iced tea.

"Dessert is ice cream sandwiches," Gary announced when they finished. "Quincy knows where to find them."

She went to the kitchen and took three from the freezer. When they had been eaten and she started to clear the table, Delton grabbed the tea glasses. "I'll help."

"If you'll bring things to me, I'll load them in the dishwasher."

When they finished tidying up and joined Gary in the living room, he was ready to leave. "I'll drive." He rolled to the door and opened it.

At his van, he hoisted himself from the wheelchair into the driver's seat with the ease of long practice. "I'll put this in the passenger seat," he said, grabbing the chair and folding it before either of them could get to it. "You two will have to sit in the back."

Quincy gave Delton a look acknowledging that might have been a calculated move by Gary and to not let it bother him. His response was a silent chuckle that made his throat jiggle.

The drive only took ten minutes. When she and Delton followed Gary's wheelchair into the nursing home, Quincy scanned the lobby and dining room. "She's sitting over there." She pointed toward the right side of the lobby where the TV resided.

At that moment, Jocelyn turned in her wheelchair, as if alerted by the sounds of them entering. Her eyes widening in recognition, she wheeled her chair around. She wore a simple blue house dress and had a fleecy throw blanket over her lap against the cool of the air conditioning. Wisps of white hair framed her wrinkle lined face.

As she rolled toward them, Gary rolled to meet her so fast Quincy feared they would collide. But, excellent drivers that they were, they halted practically toe-to-toe facing one another.

Gary reached over and placed his hands over one of Jocelyn's. "I wanted to meet you and tell you how much we loved Quincy all these years."

"You're her ..." Jocelyn halted, her voice quavering.

"I'm Gary Clark. My wife and I adopted Quincy when she was a little thing, and she changed our lives, brightened it beyond belief."

Jocelyn glanced around.

"My wife died two years ago," he explained. "That's when I encouraged Quincy to search more actively for any birth family she might have."

The woman looked at their side-by-side chairs and grinned. "Thank you for loving and taking good care of my niece. We're a nice pair of hot wheeling geezers, aren't we?"

"We sure are."

Jocelyn shifted her gaze to Quincy. "Have you made any more headway?"

"Let's move over by that sofa," Gary said, nodding at the one against the four-foot high partition behind the lobby.

When Delton and Quincy were seated facing the hot wheeling seniors, he spoke. "Just this morning I went to the bank with a warrant to see records of any accounts or safety deposit boxes your sister and her husband had. The bank manager spoke with me and printed information that included the contents of the lock box. It had some jewelry and a few other items in it. There was also a life insurance policy that has no cash value left. Their checking account, savings account, and the box contents were all turned over to the state as unclaimed property. There's no time limit on claiming it," he added.

"Oh, Quincy should do that," Jocelyn said instantly.

"The house is yours, though," Quincy said. "You paid the mortgage. I'm sure property is meant to be claimed from deceased relatives, and I'm not ready to accept that yet.

There's no proof even if I was," she added.

Jocelyn frowned. "Have you spoken to Janet and Drake's business partners?"

"We have," Delton confirmed. "They both said they have no idea where your sister and her brother-in-law went."

Quincy and Delton backed away from the conversation a bit, watching and listening as Jocelyn and Gary chatted and got acquainted. Their obvious pleasure warmed Quincy's heart.

When Gary announced he was ready to leave, they said their good-byes, promised to keep in touch, and headed for the door.

Once Gary was settled behind the wheel of his van, he glanced out at where she and Delton stood beside him. "I have an urge to see where Quincy's staying. Do either of you mind if I grab a change of clothes from my house and then follow you to Branson and sleep in my camper? I'd just like to get out of town for a bit—and see if Quincy has been taking care of my house on wheels," he added jokingly. "You did say it's at that house where you're staying, didn't you?"

Before Quincy could form a response, Delton said, "I've been sleeping in it, but an extra set of ears and eyes would be welcome. You have two beds in it."

Gary aimed a thumbs-up over his shoulder, shut the door, and started the engine.

Within minutes they had driven to the house, Gary had gone inside for an overnight bag, and they were on the road to Branson. Quincy had meant to ride with Gary, but Delton had insisted she stay in his vehicle under his guard. Gary tailed them, but fell behind when traffic increased.

"Is your work schedule the usual in the morning?" Delton asked as they rolled into Branson.

"Yes. But do you really think it's necessary for you to take me?"

"It is," he stated firmly. "It's that or quit the job."

She said no more. When he turned into the Fullers' driveway, the glare of the truck's headlights bounced off the garage door. A streetlight gleamed faintly from down the street. She peered across the dark lawn. "It looks like Logan and Dana aren't home."

Delton opened his door, causing the dome light to illuminate his face. "Logan mentioned a tee ball game for his son and something else for the daughter. So they've gone in separate vehicles to different places."

Lights beamed from a vehicle approaching from up the street. "That must be Dad," Quincy said, not surprised to see it moving at such a slow speed. But then she realized it wasn't a van.

Before she could assimilate any more, the dark colored car edged to the curb across the street. Then, simultaneously, she saw something poke out through the car window, and a loud crack of sound ripped the night.

Delton threw himself toward her, shouting, "Get down!"

Chapter 11

The gunshot had barely registered when it was followed by the sound of screeching tires. Then another shot was accompanied by the sound of shattering glass. And more tire squealing sounded from across the street.

Delton raised his head to peer out the driver's door window, one hand pressing on Quincy's shoulder to make sure she stayed down. Gary's van had stopped behind them at an angle, and the vehicle across the street was peeling away.

"Call 911," he said to Quincy, shoving the door open and scrambling outside. He ran to Gary's vehicle. The man sat behind the wheel, his window rolled down.

"Whatever you did, thanks, pal."

Gary pushed his head out the opening. "I was coming up behind that slow moving car when I saw it pull over and a rifle barrel poke out the window. I yanked my gun—I have a permit—from the glove compartment and shot at it. I think I hit the rear window. Too bad it wasn't the front one."

As he finished his rushed explanation, the shrill wail of a siren reached them. Moments later a police car came racing up the street and screeched to a halt at the curb. Officer Schofield emerged and loped to them. When he recognized

Delton, he scanned the van and car. "What's going on here? Isn't this Fuller's place?"

"It is. He's not home. Someone took a pot shot at us as we arrived."

"Who's we?"

Delton jerked his head toward his pickup where Quincy was just emerging. "Quincy Clark and me. We've been staying here with Logan."

Schofield, a middle-aged veteran, nodded. "I know about the case. Tell me your story."

By now Gary had exited his van into his wheelchair and joined them. After they each gave their statements and Schofield had made his notes, he tucked his notepad back into his pocket and faced Delton. "You should call the chief and let him know about this. I could do it, but I think he'd like to hear it from you."

"I'll do that."

When the officer left, Delton looked down at Gary in his wheelchair. "I'm thankful you were here and for your quick intervention."

"Timing," Gary replied. "God had to have timed it for me to be in exactly the right place at the right time."

The man's confident response made Delton's spine stiffen. He had become jaded by the bad things he had seen in his line of work. He uttered a prayer on occasion from habit, but he'd been struggling for years with a lack of spiritual assurance. He knew God existed and loved people, but he didn't feel His presence like he had when he was a child. But he sensed that God had truly had something to do with this incident.

"I hadn't thought about that, but I believe you're right. Has God told you anything else?"

Gary shrugged. "He gave me common sense, and it's telling me that Quincy isn't safe here at your friend's house any longer."

Delton turned to face her arms-across-the-chest stance.

"He's right. I'm guessing there's a tracking device on your van. It's parked around back near the camper," he explained to Gary. "I not only think she has to find another place to stay, but she needs to quit her job. The shooter knows where she works and apparently her schedule."

She stared at him in silence for several long moments, and then a few more at her dad, whose head was bobbing that she should do it. Finally, she sighed in resignation. "Okay. But I don't know my boss's phone number."

"We can run by the Homestead and ask the security guard to call the right person and let you explain the situation. But first I want to look at your vehicle."

"After you check it, I'll follow you to her workplace," Gary said. "The camper and her van can stay here. But she can't. She and I can get a motel room. Or how about I get two adjoining ones and you and I share one of them?"

Delton considered for only a moment. She had to move, and he needed to stick close to her. "Will you let me pay half?"

"Suit yourself. Let's check that van."

As expected, Delton found a tracking device on the van. The shooter must have bugged it before she moved it here, when she last drove it to work, and had been watching for her to appear. He called Logan to explain why he wouldn't be there that night. Then they set out.

They took care of the job termination first, and then drove to a motel outside of town.

"I'll register," Gary said when they emerged from their vehicles that were parked side by side and met in front of them. "My name isn't known to whoever is after Quincy."

"Don't use your credit card," Delton said. "I don't think so, but let's exercise caution in case that shooter managed to get your license plate number and can identify you."

Gary nodded and pulled out his wallet. "I think I have enough cash."

"I have some," Quincy offered.

"I think I have about two hundred on me," Delton said. "Let's request a room on the back side of the building."

The older clerk accepted their cash after being shown Delton's badge and realizing he was with the local department. "There's complimentary breakfast here in the morning, if you're interested."

They thanked her and went back to their vehicles. Delton and Quincy waited until Gary was behind the wheel of his van before getting into Delton's pickup.

He followed the van to the back and parked near their adjacent rooms. He would have preferred to park further away, but Gary needed close access to his vehicle in case they had to leave in a hurry. And he couldn't let anything happen to the man. Not only was he Quincy's dad, but he had sped to their rescue without hesitation.

Gary rolled ahead of them into the motel room Delton unlocked. "I'll take that bed," he said, pointing at the one nearest the hallway. "There's more room for my chair over here."

Delton grinned at the man's take charge manner. He was right. And Delton certainly didn't mind being over near the window with a view of the parking lot.

Gary tossed his bag onto the bed and rotated the chair to face them. "Who do you two think is out to kill Quincy?"

When Quincy dropped onto the chair in front of the desk, Delton grabbed the one at the end of it, turned it around, and sat with his arms draped over the back of it. What would it feel like to reach over and touch her face? He shook off the thought that had sneaked up on him.

"It's whoever did something to her parents, but we haven't figured out the identity yet."

"We've spoken to some people who knew them," Quincy said.

"It's someone who's tech savvy," Delton continued. "That tracking device on Quincy's van that led him to my friend's house is quite sophisticated."

"I'm glad you insisted on driving your vehicle to Springfield," she said, giving him a look of gratitude.

He met it steadily and grinned. "I'm always right, huh?"

Something like a groan came from Gary. "Knock it off, you two." But his tone sounded more amused than irritated.

"I wish I knew how to track my parents' car—and their furniture," Quincy said, rubbing a hand across her forehead.

Delton nodded. "They've been gone an awfully long time, but maybe I can locate a moving company with records dating back that far. It's worth a try."

"What about that theater? Now that the owner knows he was hoodwinked with that deed, he might be more forthcoming—or willing to look for information."

"Good thinking. And Mrs. Scranton might remember more details about the gambling now that we know Romano is dead."

"Well, it sounds to me like you two have busy plans," Gary said. "But I'm exhausted. If I get some sleep and go home in the morning, will you take good care of Quincy?" he asked Delton.

Delton nodded. "I'll do my best."

"I'd rather have her with me, but you can move faster than I can, and I think you have a vested interest, so I figure she's safer here."

Delton ignored the innuendo. "I'll open the connecting door, and she can keep it open." He accompanied her into the room and gave it a quick visual inspection.

"I need some clothes from the camper," she said, dumping her purse on the desk. Then she faced him. "Dad's right about me being safer here, but it's also where the answers are. And I want to go with you tomorrow."

"I don't think you should. You're not in law enforcement. I've already taken you with me more than I should have."

"I enforce school regulations with teenagers, which is not always easy," she pointed out. "I might be able to pick up on details you don't. And I don't want to stay cooped up here while you're out there hunting answers for me. Let me go."

He didn't respond for a moment, debating the wisdom of it. She had proven she had a good head on her shoulders. He wasn't absolutely sure she would stay behind where she was told, and having her with him meant he could be sure of her whereabouts. "Okay, let's go."

He also needed a change of clothes. And another thing worried him. What if they found out that her parents really had been involved in illegal dealings all those years ago?

~

Right after Quincy and the guys had a quick breakfast in the dining area of the lobby the next morning, Gary left for home. After watching him drive out of the parking lot, they got into Delton's pickup.

"I checked to make sure there's no tracker on my truck before you and your dad finished eating," Delton said. "It's clean. Let's go."

Back at the Fuller house, the family had already left for the day. Quincy was glad because it meant they didn't have to answer questions for which they had no answers. Delton accompanied her inside the camper and waited while she packed a bag. Then he insisted that she go with him to get his own bag from inside the house rather than wait out in the open for him.

Minutes later they headed back to Mrs. Scranton's house. The woman's expression registered surprise when she opened her door in response to Delton's ring. "I haven't remembered any more since talking to you," she said, stepping out onto the porch rather than inviting them inside.

Quincy swallowed against disappointment.

"We were hoping you would remember more about the gambling," Delton said. "Didn't you work at the theater a long time?"

"Twelve years," she said, lines forming across her brow.

"Didn't you hear rumors?"

She shrugged. "Sure. But I didn't pay a lot of attention. I had a full-time job and kids to take care of at home. I didn't have time for gossip."

Quincy liked that. "What kind of people came to the casino?"

The woman's mouth did a little twist. "Based on the fancy cars I saw in the lot, I assume they were well-to-do."

"What about Mr. Romano? Was he alone or with people when you saw him?"

She frowned in concentration. "Come to think of it, he was usually with Allen Ramsey or another man I didn't know. I guess none of them are still around. I haven't seen any of them for years."

"Mr. Romano is dead," Delton said bluntly.

She made a little startled movement. "I didn't know that. Of course, I've been retired for a few years and don't keep up with much of that kind of news."

"Well, thank you for your time."

Chapter 12

The Heartland Hoedown Theater, as expected, was not open to the public so early in the day. But knocking on the glass front door and Delton flashing his badge got them inside.

"We need to speak to Mr. Carruthers," he told the maid they had met on their previous visit.

She pointed to his office. "He's in there."

Delton tapped on the door and entered, with Quincy right beside him. He knew he shouldn't have her with him, but he liked having her there—for more than just safeguarding.

Carruthers looked up from whatever he was reading and frowned in recognition. Delton couldn't blame him for not being happy to see them.

"What have you dug up now?" the man asked in a not particularly welcoming tone. "Haven't you caused me enough trouble?"

Quincy darted across the room to his desk. "That was never our intent. I simply want to find out what happened to my parents. I can't apologize for that."

His scowl dissipated somewhat. "My anger is not with you, Ma'am. It's with that piece of dirt, Allen Ramsey."

She nodded. "I understand."

Delton knew that she did. He did, too.

"I've reported the forgery to law enforcement and retained a real estate attorney," Carruthers said, easing back in his plush chair. He made a hand motion for them to take the chairs in front of the desk.

They did. "Our investigation has led to the fact that there was a casino operating in the basement of this theater before that couple sold it to you," Delton informed the man. "Were you aware of that?"

A look of consternation crossed his face. His head moved slowly back and forth, and his hand raked over his eyes. Delton's gut read his reaction as innocence of such knowledge.

Carruthers removed the hand and stiffened his posture. "If that's so, something must have gone wrong. Maybe the other couple took off with their money." His gaze landed on Quincy, realizing he had accused her parents. "Or something happened to them and the other couple covered it up. That makes more sense now that I think about it."

Quincy edged up on the seat. "I'm not prepared to accept that my parents cheated their partners and ran away, leaving their baby behind. I think something happened to them. And I'd like to find out what it was—and where they are."

Carruthers stared at her for several moments. Then he leaned forward on his arms and pulled in a long breath. "I understand. But I don't know what I can do to help you. This has all hit me like the proverbial ton of bricks."

Delton welcomed the opening for his request. "Running a casino requires workers. Do you happen to have any old employee records still around in storage somewhere?"

The man's brow creased in concentration. "I'm not sure. Records that old may have been dumped. But …" he added and paused before continuing. "We have an older employee who might know where to find records that old if we have them. Let me make a call."

Delton flashed a smile at Quincy when he saw hope brighten her eyes. They waited while Carruthers spoke to someone and asked if a list of employees from the year he bought the theater was available.

When he ended the call, he focused on them. "Buddy worked in the business office back then and knows where to find anything I need. Would you like something to drink while we wait to hear from him?"

"No, thanks." Delton looked at Quincy. "How about you?"

She shook her head. "I don't need anything."

Delton stood. "You're a busy man, and we appreciate how helpful you've been. We'll wait out in the lobby so you can get back to your work."

Carruthers nodded. "I'll tell Buddy where to bring you a copy of whatever he finds."

They exited the office and settled on a bench seat in the lobby. But before they could develop a conversation, an older gentleman came toward them from the hallway on the opposite side of the lobby from the one where Carruthers' office was located.

"The boss said you want this," the portly, gray haired man said, halting before them and extending a flat folder to Delton. His eyes darted over them and lingered a few seconds on Quincy.

They both stood as Delton accepted the folder and opened it. A quick glance showed him a column of employee names, positions and addresses.

It felt like progress. He hoped something jumped out at them from this list.

~

As Delton drove past a Burger King, he realized his stomach was talking to him. "Are you hungry enough to eat a whopper?"

Quincy brightened. "It sounds good. Could we take it to

a roadside park?"

"Sure." He smiled, liking the idea, and pulled into the parking lot. Within minutes they had burgers and sodas, and he was back behind the wheel.

A few miles later, he turned in at a roadside rest stop. When he braked to a halt, Quincy grabbed the food bag while he got the drinks.

They settled at one of the two picnic tables, and she spoke a blessing. They enjoyed the unexpected privacy of the unoccupied space and the beautiful day as they ate.

When they finished, Quincy inhaled deeply and turned to gaze out over the wooded valley to their right. "How can anyone see and smell all this beauty and not be thankful to God for it?" she asked, as if speaking to herself.

He stared at the scene. "Yes, I believe God created it, but I'm not sure where He is. I mean, He seems so remote."

She turned to face him. "He's our loving heavenly Father, and He's watching over us every moment. If we need His help, all we have to do is ask."

"You really believe that, don't you?"

She nodded. "I really do. My parents taught me that from the time they adopted me, but I also studied the Bible and prayed about things for myself. And I've asked Him to help us find the answers we're seeking."

His brain jumped track slightly. "Did it bother you when you found out you were adopted?"

She placed a hand around her drink cup and began to move it back and forth with a finger. "It shook me at first. I hadn't suspected such a thing. I was only eight, and after that I felt that I had been abandoned by my biological parents. But when my adoptive parents pointed out that Jesus was adopted by Joseph, and Moses was adopted by Pharaoh's daughter, I felt like royalty. As I grew older, I realized that when we put our lives in God's hands, we become His adopted children."

Her words touched him. "It sounds like you had a good

set of parents."

She smiled. "I did. What about you? Were you and your parents close?"

"I was four and Darlene two when our dad left. He never came around anymore and became a vague memory. My mother had to work long hours to support us, so Darlene and I were left on our own a lot. She was a good kid, but I started keeping company with a rather wild crowd when I was a teen."

Quincy's eyes narrowed, studying him. "You seem to have turned out all right."

"I got in some trouble, and Mom made some changes. She found ways to be with us more and began taking us to church. I found a new set of friends there. I still feel some guilt over my bad behavior, but I credit Mom for recognizing my needs and doing something about it. We're close, even though I don't see her as often as I should."

"Like many children in your situation, you may have felt that you were the reason your dad walked out on his family." Her voice oozed understanding.

Their gazes locked. "You're right. To this day I don't understand why he married and had children if he didn't want them. And I may still feel a touch of blame. But I never doubted Mom's love for us, even though life was hard."

"But you wondered what life would have been like if you had two parents," she said in soft empathy. "Like I wondered what life would have been like if my birth parents had raised me."

He shrugged. "How about we go hunting, see if we can find out what happened to your parents' furniture?"

They spent the afternoon checking with moving companies, visiting the ones nearby and calling ones in the surrounding areas. None of them could find any record of having moved a family by that name or during that time.

Delton stared over the steering wheel rather than starting the engine after their last stop, debating what to do next. "Let's visit that neighbor of the Claytons that the woman living in Jocelyn's house said saw the furniture being loaded.

~

Quincy's discouragement returned when they finished speaking to that neighbor. The woman hadn't been able to tell them anything other than she thought the truck had been big and white with orange or red lettering on it.

"It sounds like a U-Haul truck to me," Quincy said, staring across the lawn at the house where her parents had lived. A sense of loss and desolation crept through her. Where had they been all these years?

"I need to check in at the police station."

Delton's statement jerked her from her reverie. She faced him. "Your captain has been good about you spending so much time on this case. I'm sure there are others needing your attention."

"But none as urgent. And it's one I had worked on a little bit in my own department before being borrowed down here. It's working out well."

And to her advantage. She thanked God for that.

It took about twenty minutes to navigate the streets and pull into the parking lot at the police station. The sun gleamed brightly from overhead as they exited the pickup. In her peripheral vision, Quincy saw a man emerge from an SUV near the lot entrance. She thought nothing of it, until his pace picked up and he walked up closer behind them. Then she hauled in a full breath as she recognized him.

"I think Carruthers called that man Buddy," she said softly. Delton nodded and turned to greet him. "Hello, Sir. Did you want to speak to us?"

Buddy stopped next to them. "I do," he said in a wheeze, his portly body heaving from the exertion of the short trek. His head swiveled in a furtive sweep of the parking lot.

They waited while he caught his breath.

"I worked at the theater back when the Clayton and

Ramsey couples owned it," he said after a few moments, breathing a little steadier now. "What's it worth to you to know about the doin's in that place back then?"

Delton's mouth tightened. "If you were involved, it might be worth not doing time for it."

Buddy's face went slightly paler. Then he pulled a folded piece of paper from his pocket and shoved it at Delton. "This is another employee list. It's for the casino. And there was more than just gambling going on in there."

Quincy studied the man, trying to read him. Why was he handing over such information? He didn't strike her as a person with altruistic motives. To have such information meant he had to have been involved. Didn't it?

"Are you going to tell us what it was?" Delton asked.

Buddy darted another furtive look toward the highway. Then he nodded. "They were laundering money."

At that moment a speeding car veered into the parking lot and raced toward them. As it sped closer, a gun appeared in the open passenger window and began firing.

"Get down!" Delton shouted, shoving both Quincy and Buddy to the ground and shielding them with his own body as much as he could.

As the car screeched around the lot and roared away, Quincy heard a moan next to her. She looked up to see Delton leap to his feet and pull his gun. But he lowered it as the car zoomed back onto the highway and merged into traffic. He dropped back to his knees beside Quincy. "Are you all right?"

She nodded. "But I don't think Buddy is."

Before her brain could unscramble enough to call 911, officers came spilling out of the police station. She saw one run to the edge of the lot and peer up the street while another dropped to the pavement next to Buddy and Delton. "Call an ambulance," he ordered loudly while checking the bleeding man's chest.

~

"Who was the target?" Chief Crenshaw asked, scanning the surveillance footage they had watched over and over. "Quincy or Buddy?"

Delton grimaced. "My gut says both. Whoever is out there is getting bolder—and desperate."

Crenshaw shook his head. "I agree. And there's an accomplice. Someone drove that car for the shooter, like the incident at Fuller's house. To do what they did, where they did, tells me two things. One, they're still after Quincy. Two, they somehow knew Buddy was going to give you information and were frantic to stop him."

"The license plate on that car was covered," Delton muttered, staring at the paused film. If they're panicking, they'll make a mistake."

The chief's eyes narrowed. "I'll approve whatever overtime you need to stay on this."

"I need to get Quincy to another safe place, but nowhere seems safe."

"Take care of that first. Then come back and start digging into files and the internet. Find out all you can about Buddy, the names on that list, and what was going on in that theater back then. It has to be relevant."

Delton stood and started to leave, but paused. "Have you heard anything about Buddy's condition?"

The chief's face was grim. "It's not good. His chances are slim. I'll let you know if I hear of any change—good or bad. Now go keep the gal safe."

Delton found Quincy in his office where he had left her. "We have to find another place for you to stay."

She looked him in the eye. "You don't have to do that."

"Do you have something in mind?"

Chapter 13

Quincy took a deep breath, grasping for an idea. "I don't like bouncing around like this, but I can't go to Dad's and put him at risk. And I'm sure whoever is after me know where my apartment in Springfield is by now."

She turned and stared out the window. As she did, a possibility came to mind. She spun on her heel, retrieved her purse from Delton's desk, and dug out the note with Holly Lindstrom's phone number on it.

Ignoring Delton's questioning look, she dialed the number, and then looked at him as it rang. "I'm calling my mother's friend."

He nodded approval.

"Hello?"

Quincy had trouble formulating her request when Holly answered. "Uh, this is Quincy Clark," she said haltingly.

"Oh, hello, Quincy. It's so good to hear from you. Is there anything I can do for you?"

"Well, um, I seem to have a problem."

"I know someone attacked you since we met. Has something else happened?"

"Yes. And I don't know how to ask this, but could you …"

"Do you need a place to stay?" Holly asked when she hesitated.

"Yes," Quincy said, relieved at the woman's quick grasp of the situation. "I don't want to cause you any trouble, but I need a place to stay out of sight."

"Then you've called the right person. We're out of town in a secluded area." As she gave directions, Quincy repeated them to Delton. "How soon should I expect you?"

"We'll head that way immediately," Delton said loud enough for Holly to hear.

Minutes later he drove up a long, inclined driveway to a fairly new looking ranch style home and stopped before the two-car garage.

The door slid up to reveal Holly Lindstrom and a man Quincy assumed was her husband. They pointed to the empty side of the garage, and Delton pulled into the space.

"Larry moved his car around back so you could park in here," Holly said as they emerged from Delton's pickup. Dressed in jeans and a loose green top, her shoulder length dark hair swirled about her neck. Sincerity colored her voice.

Larry introduced himself, took Quincy's overnight bag from Delton, and headed down a hallway with it.

"I need to get back to the police station and work on the case," Delton said, scanning the layout. "Thank you for helping out like this."

"Oh, we're thrilled to do it," Holly said, hugging Quincy. "You run along, and don't worry about your girl."

Quincy drew back and peeked over at Delton. To her surprise, he shot her a wink. Then he turned and left.

"Don't bother denying there's a spark between you two," Holly said as he disappeared. "Now let's sit down with some iced tea while you tell me what's happening."

Quincy followed her to the kitchen and accepted the tea she poured. Then they returned to the living room where Larry now sat in a recliner.

"So you had to quit your job," Holly said when Quincy

had given them a summary of the past few days. She and Larry had put her at ease as they talked. Holly seemed to have been a dear friend of Janet Clayton and still loved Quincy.

Larry and Holly's four children were grown and married, but the couple still worked part-time, Larry at their hardware store a son now managed, and Holly at the post office.

"There didn't seem to be any choice," Quincy said, wincing. "I feel bad about it, but Delton says it's too dangerous for me to continue, and I don't want to cause risk to anyone at the company."

"You did the right thing," Holly assured her. "I work mornings, but I'll be home in time to have lunch with you tomorrow."

"I don't know his last name, but do you remember a Buddy working at the theater?" Quincy asked, knowing it was a long shot.

Both Larry and Holly frowned. Larry shook his head. "The name doesn't sound familiar."

"I wonder what his real name is," Holly said. "Surely Buddy is a nickname."

"That's a good point." But one they couldn't answer. "What about that argument you overheard the partners of my parents having. Have you thought any more about it?"

Holly nodded. "I have, but I can't recall what was being said. I just know they were yelling. I even heard a thud that made me think one of them had thrown something. But I only know they sounded like they were fighting, the way couples do when one of them has been unfaithful—or something like that," she added, the words trailing off as if too unpleasant to have said aloud.

The next thing Quincy knew, Holly had scooted over next to her on the sofa and gripped her hands. "Let's pray about it."

Knowing that she was under the roof of people who

would pray for her gave Quincy a strong measure of peace.

~

Delton stifled a yawn as he settled back in front of his computer at the police station the next morning. There had to be significant information about Buddy. But he didn't know the man's full name. He hadn't thought to ask.

Rather than bother Mr. Carruthers, he opened a desk drawer and pulled out the employee list Buddy had given them at the theater. He read through the names. When he found a Buddy Edwards on it, he turned back to the computer, hoping the man had a profile in the system.

The first thing he found of interest was that the man's real given name was Buford.

The only criminal records he found were ones for driving under the influence and a conviction for being a bagman for a bookie during the time the theater was owned by the Clayton and Ramsey couples. The man had not lost his job over the conviction, leading Delton to believe he had been working for the casino as well as the theater.

His gut tightened anew at the possibility of having Quincy learn that her parents had been involved in criminal activities. He hoped that would not be proven true.

He located a news article about Buddy's arrest. It was brief, but it revealed that another guy had been arrested as well. Delton checked the name Arnold Grierson and found no family connection between the two men, but there was an Arnie Grierson on the casino employee list.

He spent the rest of the morning searching for and devouring everything he could find about either of the two men. He found only a couple of brief articles about incidents at the theater that involved police visits to arrest troublemakers. But it was enough to convince him that Buddy and Arnie had been cronies.

With that in mind, Delton went about trying to determine Arnie's whereabouts. But the guy had dropped out of sight. And that led to speculation.

Had they been partners in crime? Had Arnie stiffed Buddy and taken off with whatever big payoff they had made? If so, Buddy's motive in turning in that list could be revenge.

That led to more questions. What kind of payoff would have been big enough for such a break? Was Arnie the shooter?

Another horrible possibility came to mind. Could the two have received a big fee for getting rid of the Claytons? If so, silencing Buddy would certainly be a priority now that he was apparently ready to spill everything.

When Delton glanced at the clock and saw it was lunch time, he decided to go check on Quincy and see if she had eaten. After telling the chief his plans, he left his pickup in the lot and drove an unmarked car to the Lindstrom home. On arriving, he studied the scenic hillsides in the background and estimated that Holly's home was only a couple of miles from the Clayton home. The beauty of the wooded hills never ceased to impress him. He felt better about Quincy's safety now that she had quit her job and was here with friends who had known her parents.

He rang the doorbell with anticipation. He was anxious to see how Quincy was handling her situation—and was pleased when she was the one who opened the door.

He thought he detected strain in her smile. She wore jeans with a loose cotton top and white sandals. "Holly's home for lunch and we're ready to eat," she said as Holly appeared behind her.

Holly beckoned toward the kitchen. "Come on and have some broccoli cheese soup and crackers and a salad with us."

He joined them at the table. Holly offered a blessing, and they tackled the food. When Delton finished and placed his napkin and fork next to his empty soup bowl, Quincy faced him. "Have you found any more leads?"

"Buddy's proper name is Buford Edwards. He and a guy named Arnie Grierson each have an arrest record for acting as bagmen for a bookie. Arnie, possibly a pal, is on that casino employee list. And I can find no trace of him."

She and Holly both frowned, but Quincy spoke while Holly began unobtrusively clearing the table. "Are you saying you think they were involved in the gambling operation?"

"The fact that the name is so obvious on the list Buddy gave us makes me think they were—and he meant for me to see it."

"Just before he was shot, he mentioned money laundering," she said in slow thought.

"It's only a theory, but I think they were in on that—and more on the side. And I'm betting," he grinned as he used the term, "they made big bucks and built a nice stash."

"Then the partner took off with the money," she finished the theory for him. "Since this Arnie is still invisible, do you think Buddy's motive is to get the police to find him?"

"I think Buddy plans to testify against him, figuring the money's long gone, so putting the guy in prison is the most revenge he can hope for now."

"You said more. What else do you think they were doing?"

He heaved a deep breath, not comfortable with sharing this suspicion, but knew she would arrive at the same possibility sooner or later. "I think it's possible they could have done something to your parents."

She went motionless, her eyes rounding as she absorbed the idea.

"Would you like to go for a ride?" he asked.

Her head nodded in swift jerks.

"Do you have a big hat and sunglasses you could wear?"

"I have some if she doesn't," Holly offered, giving the table a final swipe with a dishcloth.

~

Quincy's mind swirled as she scooted into the car Delton had parked in the driveway. She straightened the wide brimmed hat that had nearly toppled off her head when it brushed the top of the door frame.

"How would money laundering have worked? I mean, I know it's running dirty money through legitimate businesses to clean it. But how does it fit here?"

Delton drove into the street. "Casinos are favored by criminals because huge cash flows are normal in them. They accept people with bad reputations and welcome and take care of high rollers. An individual can walk in and buy chips with dirty cash, play for a relatively short time, and then cash in the chips—so long as the transactions don't amount to more than ten thousand dollars."

She pondered that as he drove. Two hours later, they arrived at Allen Ramsey's home in Fayetteville. When he opened the door in response to their ring, his instant scowl made it clear he was not happy to see them. "What do you want now?" he demanded, a mulish expression on his face.

"We need to ask you about some guys who worked for you when you owned the theater," Delton said, his tone calm but tough. Ramsey's hostility ebbed somewhat, but he remained wary. And he didn't invite them inside. "Which ones?"

"Buddy Edwards and Arnold Grierson. What were their duties?"

Ramsey shrugged. "Buddy worked in the office. I think Arnie was a janitor. No, I believe he was in maintenance. That was a long time ago."

"We know they had records for working as bagmen."

"I don't remember anything about their histories," Ramsey snapped before Delton could elaborate. "They were just employees. I didn't know what they did on their own time."

"If they worked for criminals, would they have done something to the Claytons?"

"If you mean were they capable, I suppose they were, but I can't say what they would or wouldn't have done. And nobody's ever told me the Claytons are dead. They probably left the country."

"You don't think it's a possibility that someone paid those two to get rid of the couple for some reason?"

Ramsey drew back in affront. "Well, I sure didn't, if that's what you're asking. And I resent the implication."

Quincy watched and listened, studying every word and action in silence. The man seemed truthful, but he was a professional performer. And evasive. They would get no more information from him.

Delton must have agreed. With a curt nod, he turned and headed back to the car. Quincy had to fast step to keep up with him while choking on disappointment—and hanging onto her hat.

Buddy was lying in a hospital, unconscious. His partner was probably in another country, with a new identity. And Mr. Ramsey clearly didn't care or have any intention of helping locate the missing partner—or her parents.

Chapter 14

As Delton pulled into the parking lot at the police station, his phone rang. He steered into a parking spot and grabbed the phone. "Booker."

He listened to the chief's message and nearly groaned aloud. "Okay, thanks for letting me know so quickly. I'll get right on it."

He disconnected and faced Quincy's curious frown. "Buddy won't be finishing whatever he started to tell us. He just died."

"So what are you going to do now?" she asked solemnly, tension radiating from her.

He inhaled deeply. "I'm going to get a warrant and search the man's theater office and private residence for any records or evidence he might have kept. But I shouldn't have you with me."

"Don't leave me behind now," she pleaded. "I'll stay out of your way."

He looked her in the eye. "You promise?"

She nodded. "I'll even stay in the car if you want."

He didn't want to leave her alone. "We'll find a place for you to sit inside, but please don't touch anything."

As soon as he had a warrant, Delton drove to the theater

where Buddy had worked and went directly to the office of Mr. Carruthers. The man looked up when they entered.

"I just heard about Buddy," he said, shaking his head. "What do you need?"

"I'd like to search the office where he worked. He was in the police station parking lot because he waylaid us to offer us information. But he was shot before he could finish sharing it."

"I'll take you there." Carruthers stood and removed a ring of keys from his desk. Then he escorted them down the hall and stopped at a door. He flipped through the ring of keys, selected one, and unlocked the door.

Delton glanced around and spotted a chair near the door. "Miss Clark will wait out here," he said, moving the chair into the hallway next to the open doorway.

Carruthers nodded. "I'm expecting a call. Let me know if you need anything else."

Delton thanked him and approached the desk at the center of the room. After donning gloves, a search through the desk drawers and file cabinets yielded folders of contacts, miscellaneous notes and appointments, but nothing that wasn't related to the theater.

He eyed the computer at the right side of the desk and wondered if it could possibly have anything in it that dated back to the theater's previous owner. Not likely, but he sat down and did a search.

"Did you find anything?" Quincy asked when he returned in the hallway.

He shook his head. "Let's go to his residence and see if I can find anything pertinent there."

"He'd be more likely to have old and personal stuff at home, wouldn't he?" she asked as they returned to the car.

"That's what I'm hoping."

The address Delton found for Buddy turned out to be a rather run-down little frame house that reinforced his theory that Buddy had no money from past illegal dealings—

whether he had spent it or had it stolen from him by his partner.

Once inside, Quincy perched on a chair and watched while he donned gloves and began a methodical search of the room.

When he finished, he went to the bedroom and looked through the man's dresser drawers and closet. He reached up and pulled some bedding and an old shirt from the top shelf. Then he peered into the back of it and spotted a box in the back corner. He stretched up on his toes and pulled it to him.

He took it to the kitchen table and started going through it. When Quincy edged inside the room, he motioned for her to take the chair across from him.

"It looks like junk," she said, stretching her neck to watch.

Delton picked up a receipt. "It's old junk," he said, stressing the adjective. Then a flutter of hope flared at what he was seeing. "This stuff is dated in the right time frame."

She leaned forward, her attention riveted on the box. But she kept silent and didn't interfere, as promised.

He picked up another receipt and uttered a loud, "Yes!"

"What is it?"

"It's a receipt for a U-Haul truck, and it's made out to Buddy."

"He knew what happened to my parents," Quincy said in a painful moan. "And now he can't tell us."

"Maybe this can help," Delton said, staring at another piece of paper. Then his excitement grew. "This receipt is for a storage unit."

"Are we going there?"

He nodded. "As soon as I make a couple of calls. I need to let my chief know what I've found, and then I'll call the truck rental company." He could tell she was itching to go, and ignored her pacing to the door and back while he updated his superior.

While he called the truck company, she plopped back in

the chair and leaned forward, listening to his side of the conversation. As soon as he ended the call, he gave her the bad news. "They're under new ownership and have no records from that time period."

The frustration evident on her face made him want to comfort her. But he couldn't do that—not the way he wanted. His task was to keep her safe and find her long missing parents.

She left the chair and headed to the doorway as he gathered the box of papers. "Let's see if we can find that storage unit before it closes for the day." It was already four o'clock. He hoped they could make it in time.

They rode the few miles in silence, each lost in thought. When he pulled into the parking lot of a string of units, they wasted no time getting out and approaching the nearest one, ignoring the chatter and browsing taking place around them. "Where would I find whoever owns or is in charge of this place?" he asked a woman who stood near the raised doorway.

"That would be Mrs. Tucker at the end unit." She pointed at the opposite end of the row. "She has a little office in there."

"Thanks."

They made a beeline past the units, some with metal doors raised and others already closed for the day, to the last one. As they entered, an older gray-haired woman turned from the small counter where she was pouring a cup of coffee and stepped toward them. "May I help you?"

Delton pulled out his badge and the receipt and showed them to her. "Can you tell me where to find these goods?"

The woman took the receipt and peered at it, lines of puzzlement forming across her brow. "This is really old. But so am I," she added with a grin. "I have a pretty good memory, though."

When she wheeled and went to the file cabinet behind her, he followed and watched over her shoulder as she squatted and pulled out the bottom drawer.

"Some people are hoarders," she commented, running a hand over the folder tabs. "I hoard records, keep them way longer than required."

When Quincy edged up next to him, close enough to touch, Delton inhaled deeply of her clean flowery scent. He wanted to pull her to him, feel the beat of her heart next to his. When he looked over at her, he saw her pupils darken, and thought she had a similar feeling of something flowing between them. He closed his eyes for a second to break the connection.

Mrs. Tucker stood and opened the folder she had extracted from the drawer. After a quick scan, she looked up. "That unit was rented on the date of that receipt, and the rental fee was paid for a few months. Then the payments stopped, and we were unable to collect. The contents were auctioned to recoup the loss of rental fees after they had been delinquent for over a year."

~

The frustration in Delton's expression matched Quincy's own. "It feels like every time we make a step forward, it's followed by two backward."

"You're right. But we know their stuff was here," Delton said. "I've been re-interviewing people, and Mrs. Bledsoe is next on the list."

"Let's go then." She needed to keep moving, being proactive. She'd go crazy sitting around someplace wondering if any progress was being made.

She had learned to respect Delton. From what she had observed, he was good at his job. If anyone could uncover secrets that had been buried for over two decades, it was him.

Quincy watched the road and let her mind drift as he drove to the address he had located since learning more about Sharleen Bledsoe and visiting her at the theater.

They arrived at an older cottage style building at the edge of town, parked, and made their way to the porch. The door opened as they reached the step, and a man stepped outside. Tall, with wavy, gray speckled hair, he observed their approach through narrowed eyes.

"Hello, Sir," Delton said. "Are you Mr. Bledsoe?"

"I am."

Delton pulled out his badge. "I need to speak to your wife."

The man's eyes darkened in anger. "Haven't you guys hassled her enough? She told me you questioned her at the office."

Quincy wasn't sure what to make of the man's hostility. "We only want to see if she has remembered anything more about my parents," she said.

"Well, that won't happen today," he said, impatience clear in his brusque tone. "She's out of town visiting relatives."

Quincy clenched her teeth, not sure she believed him.

When Delton said, "Maybe we can catch her later," the man backed up and shut the door.

As they walked back to the car, her phone rang. The number wasn't familiar. "Hello," she said, scooting into the passenger seat as Delton opened the door for her.

"Quincy?" a male voice said.

"Yes."

"This is your Uncle Don Clayton. I found that photo album my wife made. If you'll give me your mailing address, I'll pack it up and send it to you."

"Oh, thank you," she said, delighted. "I'm staying in Branson right now, but my permanent address is in Springfield."

"You can have him send it to the police station if you'd like," Delton said, standing near enough to hear the conversation.

"What's the exact address?"

He quoted it and then went around the vehicle to get behind the wheel.

"Did you hear that, Uncle Don?" she asked into the phone.

"I got it," he said with a chuckle. "It sounds like you're with that detective." Then his tone turned sober. "I've been in contact with family members, and we're all following the stories about the things that have been happening to you."

"The detective is protecting me," she assured him.

She heard him clear his throat. "Audrey was thrilled when I told her that her dolly has been found. She can't wait to meet you."

"I'd love that. And I know my adoptive dad would love to meet both of you. I'll let you know what we find out."

They spoke a couple more minutes and ended the call. "Did you hear all of that?" she asked Delton as he drove down the street.

"Enough to follow along, but not everything."

As she finished filling in the gaps, he pulled into the parking lot of a restaurant.

Quincy's tension eased as they sat across from one another on bench seats in a dining booth and ate. Delton, on the other hand, looked pensive, almost to the point of strain.

"What's bothering you?"

He looked up from stirring his tea. "I think you need to pray that God will tell me what to do next."

She put her fork down, bowed her head, and prayed briefly but earnestly for just that.

They finished their roast beef sandwiches and headed back to the car. When he reached the passenger door first and opened it, in her rush she bumped up against him. She quickly stepped back, but her heartbeat quickened.

He studied her, that piercing gaze of his moving over her as though reading her inner turmoil. He cupped her face in a palm. "I have to put feet to that prayer, find a way to take another step forward. I'm going to take you back to Holly's and go to my office. I want to do some more research, see if I can locate Buddy's pal, Arnie."

She prayed that he would be successful. She wanted the blank holes in her family history filled—not a relationship with the man doing his best to achieve that.

Didn't she?

Could she have both, another part of her wondered? She mentally shook off the thought and refocused on the present circumstances. Could Buddy and Arnie have done something to her parents? Or was the man they had just met involved in whatever had happened to them?

Chapter 15

Delton's research on Arnie Grierson turned up an out of state address for him during the year following the disappearance of the Claytons. Was it coincidence?

He called the police department where the man had lived then and learned that Arnie had been arrested on a drunken disorderly charge and left the area after being released from jail.

His current whereabouts remained elusive. Apparently, he had gotten better about keeping a low—make that invisible—profile. If he had ever had a savings account in the area before hightailing it, that was also keeping an invisible profile.

As Delton leaned back in the chair, his stomach started growling, making him realize how late it was. He shut down the computer and headed for something to eat before going to Logan's. He wasn't going to sponge all his meals from them.

The next morning, he called Quincy and told her she should stay at Holly's, but he would try to get by to see her later in the day. Then he set out to interview anyone he could find who had known Arnie Grierson. He called on residents in the neighborhood where the man had lived, but only found one who remembered Arnie living on his block so long ago. And that one didn't know Arnie well enough to have known any work associates or personal cronies. All the man remembered about Arnie was seeing an older couple he assumed to be parents visit him occasionally.

By late afternoon, Delton was giving up hope of finding the former theater employee. Grasping for help, he sat in his police car and silently sought help from God.

When he returned to his office, he found a package on his desk addressed to Quincy from her Uncle Don. He set it back down and began a search for Arnie's parents. Eventually he found that the mother had died six years ago, the dad only two years ago. At five o'clock, he picked up Quincy's package and headed to deliver it.

~

When her phone rang, Quincy paused in scrolling the TV channels with the remote control. It was another unfamiliar number. "Hello?"

"Am I speaking to Quincy Clark?"

"Yes, you are."

"My name is Vicky Wentworth," a woman said in a tremulous voice. "I got your number from my mother, Jocelyn Rathburn."

A light flashed in Quincy's brain. "You're the one who submitted your DNA test to Ancestry."

"Yes, and I'm so glad I did. My family arrived in Branson today for some vacation time, and I'd love to visit with you if you're interested and have time for me."

"I'd *love* to meet you," Quincy said eagerly. "I'm staying with someone, but I'm sure you'd be welcome," she added, reading Holly's hand gestures from across the room.

"Tell me how to find you and I'll come straight there."

Quincy explained how to find the rural property and said good-bye, thoroughly pleased at the opportunity to meet another relative. She bubbled as she explained the connection to Holly.

Minutes later, the sound of an approaching vehicle sent her hurrying to the door. She jerked it open and stepped out onto the porch. The woman coming up the steps looked to be a few years older than her. Tall and slender, she had warm brown eyes and ash blond hair that fell in a long ponytail down her back. The stylish white top and blue slacks she wore bespoke comfort and good taste.

"I was ecstatic when Mom told me you had been found at last," she said, halting before the open door. "May I hug you?"

Quincy smiled and opened her arms. "Of course, Cousin Vicky."

After a warm embrace, Vicky pulled back and studied her. "I've wondered about you all these years. And your parents," she added. Seeing her blink back tears of joy touched Quincy deeply.

"Come inside so we can sit and visit." Quincy tugged her through the doorway. "We have a lot of catching up to do."

Holly approached, smiling. "Janet Clayton and I were close friends. If I remember correctly, you were about six or seven years older than Quincy."

Vicky stared, her eyes dancing. "You're Holly Lindstrom."

Holly nodded and opened her arms.

From that point, conversation and remembrances were shared, laughed and cried over, and time forgotten.

"How did you end up here with Holly?" Vicky asked when Holly went to the kitchen to get sodas for them.

The reminder of the attacks brought Quincy back to the present, but she schooled her features into a calm expression and gave her cousin a frank account of her time in Branson.

They became so engrossed that the sound of the doorbell startled them.

~

Delton smiled when Quincy opened the door. "This was

on my desk," he said, handing her what he assumed to be the photo album her uncle had promised.

"Oh, thank you," she said, pulling it to her. "Come in and meet Aunt Jocelyn's daughter."

He had noticed the SUV in the driveway and welcomed the opportunity to speak to another person from Quincy's newly found family.

A blond woman came toward him, hand outstretched.

"This is Detective Delton Booker," Quincy said as he shook the proffered hand. "Delton, meet Vicky Wentworth."

"Are you the person who was with Quincy when she met my mother?" the bright-eyed woman asked.

"I am. And I want to thank you for submitting your DNA for an eventual match to Quincy. I know it means a lot to her."

Quincy squeaked in delight, having opened her package. "I can't wait to see this."

She moved to the center sofa cushion and opened the album. When Vicky sat beside her, Delton sat in a rocker facing them. He nodded at Holly as she entered the room, placed cold sodas before each of them, and claimed the cushion the other side of Quincy.

He listened in fascination as the three women looked through the photo album, identifying whoever they could and speculating about others. But his gaze lingered on Quincy's delicate profile. She had a regal bearing about her, and a face that he found fascinating.

She confused him.

The emotions he felt for her were unfamiliar. She stirred him. He loved learning about her, seeing how her mind worked, and discovering her origins with her. She was an unexpected captivation he couldn't shake.

He worried about their relationship, whether there was one, or if there was, or if there should be one.

Suddenly he remembered that he had to find Arnie. And, although it was a long shot, here was someone who might remember something. He waited for a lull in the conversation, and then addressed Vicky. "Ma'am."

She met his gaze. "Yes?"

"Do you remember being around the theater when you were a girl and visited Quincy and her parents?"

Her smiling countenance turned pensive. "I remember attending Aunt Janet and Uncle Drake's show a couple of times."

"Do you remember any of the people you met there?"

"I never knew anyone personally but Quincy's parents. And it's been so long. I was only nine when they disappeared."

"So you wouldn't have known any of the theater workers."

She shook her head. "Why?"

"I'm looking for someone who worked there at the time. He was a maintenance worker."

Her brow crinkled, her expression somber. She thought for a bit before saying anything. "I remember the last time we were there, as we started to leave at the end of the show, there was a little incident, but I don't see how it could be important."

"Tell me about it anyhow."

"Someone driving a piece of machinery, I think it was a forklift, ran over an exposed cord in the front lobby. There was a lot of yelling and telling people to stay in the auditorium."

He nodded. "Running over an unprotected cord could cause the next person who touched it to be electrocuted. Did you see the driver?"

"No-o-o," she said slowly, as if struggling to picture the incident in her mind.

"It's okay. You can't be expected to remember something that vague and so long ago."

"Wait a minute," she said, snapping her fingers.

He waited while she shut her eyes, clearly searching her

memory. When she opened them, she was still frowning in concentration. "I do remember something. When they let us leave the auditorium, we headed to our car in the parking lot, and we had to stop while that forklift drove past us. My dad said something that indicated he knew the driver."

"I know it's unlikely, but do you remember if your dad mentioned a name?"

She rubbed a hand across her eyes. "He could have, but I don't remember. What's coming to me is him saying something about the man was driving like he must have gotten into his parents' bar supplies." She paused. "Then Mom asked what he meant by that, and he said they owned a bar in …I think it might have been Huntsville," she said after several moments.

"That's good," he said, wishing there had been more, but thankful for this much. "It's worth checking into."

He pushed to his feet. "I need to let you ladies continue your visit. It was nice meeting you, Vicky. And I'll be checking on the ownership of bars in Huntsville."

"Oh, don't go," the women chorused in unison.

"It's been a long day, and I need to end it. Enjoy your reunion."

Quincy followed him out onto the porch, closing the door behind her. He grasped her arm and guided her to the left of the doorway. "I'm glad you're making connections. It's late, but I'm going to talk to Logan when I get to his house and see if we can find out who owned any bars in Huntsville back then."

She gave a little nod. "Thank you for your diligence."

Without conscious thought, he tugged her into his embrace. With one hand he pushed strands of hair back from her brow and gently traced a finger over her cheek. "There's a question I'd like to ask you."

She stared at his chin. "What?"

"Are you involved with any man in particular?"

"No one special," she said softly. "I've had some men

friends, but no one serious."

"Good." He drew her to his chest and planted a kiss on her lips. Then he headed to the steps. At the first one, he turned. "I'll call you tomorrow."

He drove, whistling under his breath, to Logan's house.

"What are you looking so smug about?" Logan asked when Delton entered the living room.

Delton shrugged, and avoided the question. "I have a task for us."

Logan chuckled. "Us, huh?"

Delton shrugged. So, what if he meant a task for the tech guru.

After supper they went to Logan's office. Within a half hour his friend had identified a bar in Huntsville that had been owned by a couple by the name of Grierson. And they had a son named Arnold.

Chapter 16

Delton was just starting to undress for a shower when his phone rang. He grabbed it from the dresser where he had laid it. He didn't recognize the number. "Hello?"

"This is Gary Clark, and I'd like to ask a favor."

He made a quick mental guess that Quincy's dad wanted something related to his daughter's safety, but he asked anyhow. "What do you need?"

"Tomorrow is Quincy's birthday. At least, it's the day we always celebrate based on the note found in her infant seat. We only missed the exact date shown on the birth certificate she found after the DNA matches by three days."

"And you want to take her to a nice restaurant," Delton said, the man's intent dawning. "I think it's great of you, but I'm not comfortable taking her out in public. Would you consider meeting us at my house in Springfield, which shouldn't be on the shooter's radar, and letting me have food brought in at my expense?"

Moments of silence elapsed. "How about this? I know her favorites, so I'll take care of the food, and you sneak a birthday cake into your vehicle."

Delton grinned. "It's a deal. What time do you want us to meet you there?"

"If you can make it by five-thirty, I'll schedule food delivery for six. But I need the address of your house."

After giving it to him and ending the call, Delton debated how to approach Quincy the next day. He called her.

"I need to spend tomorrow morning at the office and running a couple of errands," he said when she answered. "Then I'll be driving to Huntsville to look for Mr. Grierson. If you want to ride along, I'll pick you up right after lunch."

"Of course, I want to ride along," she responded without hesitation.

"Okay, look for me about twelve-thirty. We'll plan on eating out on our way home."

"That sounds good."

As he disconnected and continued to the shower, he made plans to stop at a bakery for a birthday cake and a florist for some flowers on his way to the station in the morning. He would stash them at Logan's on the excuse of swapping his police vehicle for his pickup and find a way to sneak them into it before driving to Springfield.

~

The next day, Quincy stopped pacing the floor while waiting to hear from Delton. She snatched her phone when it rang. It had been raining lightly all morning, the gloominess and pattering on the roof adding to her low spirits.

Such a day didn't usually bother her, but she wanted clear skies for driving today. She had her hooded windbreaker laid out and wore jeans and a comfortable blouse.

Hearing Delton say, "I'm on my way," warmed her. She donned the windbreaker and dashed out the door, glad Holly was upstairs and not observing her antsy behavior.

Outside, a ray of sun sneaking from behind the clouds made her blink in pleasure. The June of yesterday was returning.

When Delton pulled his police car into the driveway,

she yanked the passenger door open and scooted into the seat.

"I have a picture of Arnie that Logan found somewhere and printed for me. I also have two addresses," he said, easing back into the road. "I think we'll go to the bar first."

"Going bar hopping, huh?" she said with a touch of sarcasm, and then grinned.

The hour plus drive passed quickly, and it didn't take long for Delton to locate A. J.'s Bar. As they walked up the sidewalk to the dark wooded, shingled roofed building, Quincy couldn't help but wonder about the man they hoped to meet. She shivered.

"You okay?" Delton asked, noticing.

"I'm fine."

They entered and paused inside the doorway for a quick scan of the place. It wasn't exactly the Ritz. Quincy saw only three customers at tables and one at the counter. It was only mid-afternoon, so maybe business picked up in the evenings. Raucous music blasted from a radio on a shelf.

The man behind the counter was built like a bull, wide chest with a slight hunch in his shoulders, and shaggy hair that looked like it would break a comb. He peered at them in curiosity.

"I'm looking for Arnold Grierson." Delton had to speak loud to be heard over the noise.

The guy shrugged, swiping a wet cloth over the counter. "Don't know no Arnold Grierson."

Delton pulled out his badge. "Records show this place being owned by his parents until two years ago. He should have inherited it."

"I've only worked here six months. A. J. owned it then and still does."

Delton looked around the slightly run-down place, and then back at the man. Without comment, he grasped Quincy's arm and headed back outside.

"Do you think he sold the place?" Quincy asked when

they were inside the car.

"He could have, but I'm guessing not. It's a source of income and a place to live. And from what Logan saw in his financial records, he needed both."

"So, he blew whatever fortune of his and Buddy's that he theoretically took off with, and only came back here after his parents died."

"That's how it smells." He went silent, studying the screen of his phone and punching buttons.

Quincy kept quiet while he searched for something.

"A, ha," he said moments later. "Arnold's middle name is James. So the initials A. J. fit. Let's go to the residential address I have."

Minutes later he parked in front of a small frame house and faced Quincy. "I want you to wait here for me. You're in plain sight, and you don't need to be part of this."

She nodded, content to let him do his job without interference. When he knocked at the door, it swung open moments later. The man in the doorway didn't invite him inside. And he didn't look like the picture Delton had shown her of Arnie.

They spoke, and it looked like belligerence in the man's mouth and hand motions. The conversation didn't last long. The door slammed as Delton turned to return to the car.

"He's going by his initials and wearing some kind of wig, but it's him," Delton said when he was behind the wheel. "He must think he's still in hiding, which is ridiculous." He started the engine.

"What now?"

"I can't make an arrest without proof and out of my jurisdiction, but I'm satisfied it was worth the trip to confirm he's down here. I need to go by the police station to write up a report and talk to my chief. I'm not sure of Arnie's game, but my gut says he's involved in more than running a local bar."

"Do you have any ideas?"

He darted a glance at her and pulled into the street. "Considering his familiarity with the casino operation years ago at the theater, and that the former owner of that theater lives less than an hour's drive from here in Fayetteville, I'm wondering if they have another racket running."

They discussed the possibilities some more, and then became silently engrossed in their separate speculations during the remainder of the drive back to Branson. Quincy watched the light mist of rain that had come and gone all day, like her thoughts were coming and going.

She waited in the front of the police building while Delton took care of his report. He was only gone a half hour.

~

"The chief is going to have Ron work online from home and see if he can find evidence of my suspicions," Delton said to Quincy as he escorted her out of the building after finishing his reports.

"Is that the detective you're temporarily replacing?"

"It is. This could be the perfect way to get him back into harness gradually. Before we go eat, I'd like to swing by Logan's and swap this police car for my pickup."

"I don't blame you for wanting to drive your own vehicle when you're off duty. I'd feel the same if I were in your shoes."

When he parked at Logan's minutes later, he grabbed his briefcase from the trunk and put it in the back seat of his pickup. But he didn't get inside.

"I think I'll go inside and take advantage of the facilities before starting out again," he said, nodding at the house. "How about you?"

She nodded. "Good idea."

"I'll go upstairs to the guest room and leave the downstairs for you," he said as he unlocked the door. "Take your time."

When she went down the hall, he looped around to the kitchen, retrieved the cake and flowers from the fridge where he had stashed them that morning, and slipped out the back door.

Then he loped around the house to his pickup and stowed them in the back floorboard. He was just slipping back into the kitchen when he saw Quincy pass the doorway to the living room. He ducked into the hallway and entered the room as if having come down the stairs.

"Are you ready to go?" she asked.

"Yep. And I'm getting hungry. Go on and get in the truck while I lock the house."

Once back inside the vehicle, neither of them spoke until he turned onto the route to the interstate rather than continuing toward the restaurant that had been mentioned. Quincy eyed him questioningly from the passenger seat. "We wouldn't be going to my dad's, would we?"

He chuckled. "Caught, huh?" Then he explained where they were meeting Gary.

She shook her head in exasperation—while grinning. "I'm not surprised. He sent me a birthday card with a check in it, which was already overkill. But the visit will be nice. Now the question is whether we'll be having steak or lasagna."

Gary's van was parked in Delton's driveway when they arrived. And the meal turned out to be lasagna from her favorite Italian restaurant. Quincy seemed genuinely thrilled with the flowers Delton brought from the truck along with the dessert. "There's a vase under the sink."

"Those should be worth a kiss," Gary declared with a chuckle when Delton handed them to her after delivering the cake.

When a flush of red rushed over Quincy's face, Delton give her a wink. "Maybe later."

She nodded and took the flowers to the kitchen. A couple of minutes later she brought them back in a vase of water.

"All right, all right," Gary said, lifting a knife. He cut

the cake and placed slices on their dessert plates. "Now, while we eat this, I want both of you to talk to me. I want to write a story about Quincy's experience with her search for her birth parents. But I want to broaden it into an article, possibly a series if my editor likes it, about people with her kind of background and search experiences. I want to explore how they felt about their adoptions, why they set out to find their birth parents, and the eventual outcomes."

Chapter 17

Quincy looked across the table at Delton, over to her dad, and then back at Delton. The detective was distractingly handsome. To shut down her disjoined thoughts, she looked at Gary again. "I guess I shouldn't be surprised, but I hadn't been thinking about any publicity."

"Well, you've already gotten it, whether you wanted it or not," Gary said, referring to the news reports on her attacks. "So I figure we should put a positive spin on it if we can. My editor has indicated some interest, but wants a resolution to your story before going with it."

"We plan to resolve it," Delton said. "But I can't promise it'll be a pleasant outcome, only that we'll seek justice if there's been a crime."

Quincy appreciated that he didn't use the term murder. "Will you let me read it before you submit it?" she asked Gary.

"Of course." He shifted his focus to Delton. "I'd like to go over everything that's happened, in sequence, since Quincy went to work at the Homestead. I know about the search that led up to that point."

Had it only been two weeks? Quincy could hardly believe that so much had happened in such a short time.

"Humor me," Gary said, pulling a notepad and pen from the side pocket he kept attached to the arm of his wheelchair. He plopped them onto the table. "Let's go over what you know …and can share," he added, along with an eye roll.

Quincy exchanged a look with Delton. "I started working at the Homestead the first week of June," she said when he nodded. A week and a half later, I was attacked in the parking lot."

"My guess is that the attacker must have just learned of her and what she was investigating and set out to stop her from finding the answers she wants," Delton said.

"Three days later I found my birth mother's sister," Quincy continued, watching Gary as he jotted notes. "When we visited with Aunt Jocelyn, she said that her family didn't realize her sister's family had disappeared for weeks after they had last been seen. It wasn't until they discovered that their belongings had been moved from their house that she reported them missing. We didn't give her a lot of details about me being attacked after work had gotten around that I'm looking for them."

"We checked with the Department of Motor Vehicles and confirmed that their car tags and driver's licenses were never renewed," Delton continued. "Then we talked to a neighbor who saw a truck being loaded with the Claytons' furniture and belongings. We also checked on the theater deed and visited the current owner to inform him that the deed was forged. He has a lawyer pursuing that matter."

"I was shot at again, this time in your camper at the campground," Quincy said, keeping Gary's pen in motion.

"I insisted she move it to my friend's house," Delton interjected. "I can have it moved back to your place if you want."

Gary looked up from his note taking. "I don't need it right now, and you might need it again. Quincy can bring it home when she's ready to return permanently, which I hope is soon." His gaze beamed concern and love onto her.

She simply smiled, accepting and returning the feelings. Then she continued the story. "We located my birth dad's brother and heard basically the same story as my mother's sister told. After spending a night in a hotel, the detective," she hesitated to use his name, wanting to keep impressions professional, "took me to his friend's house."

Gary nodded. "The friend is a police officer, right?" When she nodded, he asked, "Is that when you finally located the former theater owners and talked to them?"

"We only met Mr. Ramsey. He and his wife divorced years ago."

"He denies knowledge of the Claytons' whereabouts," Delton explained. "The man's son was a kid back then, but when we talked to him, I got the impression he knows something he's not telling."

"Whatever it is, I think it has affected his life," Quincy said, picturing the troubled, unhappy man. "He's trying to escape with booze. He did mention a girl he used to be friends with whose mother worked at the theater."

"We talked to both," Delton continued. "The girl—woman—said she didn't remember much, but she also gave me the impression she remembers something she saw or heard. Her mother put us onto the fact that there was late night gambling going on at the theater."

"Did you ever find the former owner's ex?" Gary asked, putting his pen down and flexing his fingers.

Delton nodded. "We did, and she also denied any knowledge. They can't all be blind and deaf. After Holly came onto the scene, she gave us the name of a known gambler who was around the theater a lot. Someone was running a casino in the basement, and I'm guessing it was him."

"Did you talk to him?"

Delton shook his head. "We researched him, planning to do that, and learned that he's dead."

"When we asked Mr. Ramsey about the gambling, he

blamed my parents," Quincy blurted, frustration getting the best of her.

Delton continued. "I went to their bank and saw records of a depleted life insurance policy and that the contents of a safety deposit box had been turned over to the state as unclaimed property. Soon after that, you came to our rescue when someone shot at us at my friend's home."

Gary ignored mention of his part in the incident. "What have you learned since then?"

"We went back to the theater," Quincy said, her mind jumping ahead to what had followed. "The owner had an office worker give us a list of employees who worked at the theater before he bought it."

"The next day that man approached us on the parking lot of the police station and gave us another list. That one was of employees who worked in the casino," Delton said. "He said more was going on around there at the time, even mentioned money laundering, but before he could give us any details, a car roared into the lot and the man was shot. He was taken to the hospital, but died hours later."

Silence fell for several moments before Delton spoke again. "We searched his office and home and found a box of old receipts in the house. Among them were one for the rental of a U-Haul truck, and another for a storage unit. The truck company had no records from that long ago. The manager of the storage units found that all the belongings were auctioned for non-payment of the unit rental. And that brings us to the present."

"So who do you think is behind all this?" Gary asked, looking from one to the other of them.

~

Delton wasn't sure how much he should divulge here. They had probably already been too open. But Gary seemed to have good judgment. He was an experienced journalist with good instincts. And he had been the initiator of Quincy's quest. He seemed like the father figure Delton had never had—someone with whom could productively exchange information and ideas.

"I think the guy who may have been running the casino could have done something to the Claytons, and if he did, the Ramseys surely know about it. But they're impersonating clams, and Romano is dead."

"Does that make Mr. Ramsey a suspect?" Gary asked.

"It certainly puts him on the list."

"What about the theater worker and his pal—partner, or whatever he was—Arnie?" Quincy asked, Buddy's death apparently so fresh in her mind that the memory had her shivering.

"They had plenty of opportunity and means. And any time there's big money involved, there's motive," Delton said when Quincy went silent.

"But there's no proof?" she asked after a moment.

He shook his head. "That's right."

Gary leaned back in his wheelchair, his demeanor thoughtful. "It sounds like it's time to backtrack, take a second look at the whole case."

"I have notes in my briefcase in the truck."

"I'll make a fresh pot of coffee while you get it," Quincy said when Delton stood to leave.

Minutes later, they resettled around the table with coffee and the stack of folders—and were soon absorbed in reading through the contents.

At some point Delton noticed that Gary was staring with particular interest at one of the newspaper articles. The man leaned forward, staring at a picture in frowning concentration.

"Do you see something?" Delton knew it was the photo of the Ramsey and Clayton couples standing in front of the theater. He stood and rounded the table to peer over Gary's shoulder. Quincy did the same, her presence beside him creating a longing inside him, an intense emotion he couldn't recall ever experiencing. He gave himself a mental shake and focused on the black and white picture, examining it closely for whatever had captivated Gary.

Gary tapped a finger on the face of Allen Ramsey. "There's something about his expression. His pose is okay, but there's a tense line to his jaw, and his head is tipped sideways a wee bit. It seems to me there's a furtive look in his eyes. It gives me the feeling he's angry with someone."

Delton leaned down, wishing he could see the pupils in the man's eyes. "There could have been trouble in paradise," he mused aloud, possibilities flashing through his brain. "Ramsey admitted there was illegal gambling, but he blamed his partners."

"It's easy to blame someone else when they're not around to defend themselves," Quincy said. "I'll never believe it unless there's undeniable proof."

"We're not looking for blame right now. Let's stay focused on finding them."

"Maybe Allen and Sharleen Ramsey, or all of them, were behind it, and they were fighting over money," Gary theorized. "Money can come between people."

More possibilities came to mind. Could there have been an affair? Had the Claytons been onto something that had made it necessary to silence them? The possibilities nagged at Delton.

"Where do you go from here?" Gary asked.

"There are still more questions than answers. But I think I need to talk to Sean Ramsey and Trixie Albertson again. They were young, but kids, especially teenagers, usually perceive a lot more than their parents realize. And those two both left me with the impression that they remember something."

"Something they're afraid to tell you," came from Gary.

Delton began placing papers back in their folders.

Chapter 18

Sunday morning, Quincy was pleased to have Delton attend church with her again. The pastor's sermon about God's love for them and how they could cast all their cares on Him, gave her an inner comfort she hadn't realized how much she needed.

They ate at a nice restaurant afterward and then lingered over dessert and coffee. "Sean Ramsey will likely be working tomorrow," Delton said. "Are you too tired to go see him now?"

"Let's go." She grabbed her purse.

Dark was falling by the time they arrived at the apartment building in Rockaway Beach where Sean lived. Delton parked at the curb, and Quincy walked beside him across the street. Inside the building, they had no trouble finding the correct room number. But no one answered repeated knocks on the door.

In disappointment they retraced their way back down the hallway. When they exited the building, a thump sounded to their left. They both pivoted and scanned the verandah that was now lit by the dim glow of the porch light. Sean Ramsey sat leaning forward in a chair while raking a hand over the floor. Awkwardly he retrieved the bottle of beer he had dropped and pulled himself back upright, an almost catatonic expression on his face.

They moved that way, dragged chairs over near Sean, and sat facing him. Weaving unsteadily in the chair, he turned the bottle up and gulped the last bit of liquid from it. Then he squinted at them, blinking. "You're here again?"

In the shadow of the dim porch light behind them, Quincy watched Delton reach over and place a hand on the poor man's arm. "Yeah, it's us again. We need to explore your memories a little more."

Sean hiccupped. "You mean about all those years ago, don't you?"

Sympathy squeezed at Quincy's heart. She leaned forward, hating to take advantage of the poor guy, but hoping his inebriated state would make him more forthcoming. "Sean, I need to know whether my birth parents are alive or dead, and I think you can help us find the answer. I need to know. I don't want to live the rest of my life wondering why they abandoned me."

He just stared at her.

"Someone is trying to kill me to keep me from learning that truth," she pressed on. "You were young when my parents disappeared, but teenagers know what's going on around them, often more than their parents realize. Will you please help me? Tell me what was going on back then?"

Sean's head dropped. His hands fidgeted with the empty beer bottle, rubbing back and forth over it. Finally, he looked back up, his expression tortured. "There was a rumor of an affair between your dad and my mom," he said slowly, as if the slurred words were dragged from the pit of his being. "But she eventually married Benny, so the rumor must have been a mistake."

Delton spoke up. "You believed it at the time, though, didn't you?"

Sean made one jerky nod of his head.

"Did you confront either of them about it?"

He raised his head, glaring. "Of course not."

"So why did you believe it?"

His gaze dropped back to the bottle, rotating it in his hands. Then he heaved a breath and said, "Mom and Dad argued a lot. Then one day …"

"One day what?" Quincy asked, unable to keep quiet.

It was several long moments before Sean looked up again. "One day they came home yelling and screaming," he stammered, the words more slurred and hard to understand. "Then Mom stormed upstairs, and Dad …Dad made a …a phone call."

Suddenly his arm pulled back, and then he flung the beer bottle out onto the sidewalk.

Quincy slid to her knees and clasped her hands around his, her heart aching for whatever had caused the trauma inflicted on the young boy Sean had been. "Who did your dad call?"

He slapped his hands over his eyes. His shoulders heaved as sobs wracked them.

"Who did he call?" she repeated.

Sean swiped at his eyes. "A bud …buddy who has a construction business. He asked for a backhoe," he choked while still wiping his face.

Quincy exchanged a wide-eyed glance with Delton.

Delton cleared his throat. "Do you know what your dad did with it?"

Sean sprawled back in the chair and closed his eyes. "I did'n athk him." The low slurred words were almost indistinguishable.

"You didn't want to know?"

His head lolled sideways. "No."

"But later, when you heard the Claytons were missing, you thought you did."

Sean nodded, not opening his eyes.

"Who was the buddy with the backhoe?"

Sean opened his eyes and struggled to his feet. "Jack

Orwell." He staggered away.

Delton made no effort to detain him, so Quincy didn't either.

"I want to go with you to see the man," she said when they were back in Delton's pickup.

He considered briefly. "It's late. He won't be at work now, and I don't have a home address for him. Let's get some sleep, and I'll pick you up in the morning."

Neither of them spoke as he drove her back to Holly's house, each preoccupied with thoughts of what they had learned.

~

Monday morning, Quincy was ready and waiting in the driveway when Delton arrived. She hopped in the passenger seat. "He buried something," she said tonelessly, having come awake numerous times during the night with the thought in her mind.

"It sure looks that way." Delton put the truck into motion.

When they arrived at Orwell Construction, they found Mr. Orwell in the parking lot to their right, loading a Bobcat onto a trailer. He turned at their approach. Quincy stopped beside him to listen while Delton questioned him.

"I'm Detective Booker, and this is Quincy Clark," he said, extending a hand.

The man shook it. "What do you need?" A hint of impatience tinged his gruff voice.

"I want to ask you about the loan or rental of a backhoe to your friend Allen Ramsey over twenty years ago. Do you happen to remember such a transaction, or have records available that would verify it?"

Bushy eyebrows scrunched together. "That's a long time ago, but I dimly recall it. Allen had rental properties and sometimes borrowed equipment for doing repairs. I only charged him for it when it was for business use rather than personal."

"Do you have any idea which it was, why he needed it that particular time?"

"I didn't ask for details every time he had a property issue, and I probably loaned it to him for personal use, so there would be no record. Sorry I can't be of more help." His eye on the trailer relayed the message that he was a busy man.

Delton thanked him, and they returned to the truck. He started the engine and faced Quincy, his jawline rigid. "I didn't sleep much. I think Sean is still hiding something."

Quincy envisioned the man's shoulders heaving with sobs. "I think you're right. Are we going back to Rockaway Beach?"

"We have no choice." He pulled into the street.

Delton parked in front of Sean's apartment building minutes later. When they entered and knocked on Sean's door, there was no response at first. But when he pounded again, it swung open to reveal Sean staring at them from red-rimmed eyes, apparently unable to make it to work again, fortunately for them. With a gesture of resignation Sean motioned them inside.

"You know what your dad did with that backhoe," Delton said, not bothering to be seated. "It's time to get it off your chest."

Beside him, Quincy held her breath, unable to take her gaze off the man. She probably felt sorry for him, but she needed to hear the truth.

Sean hauled a deep breath of fatalistic acceptance. Then he stood there in silence, as if preparing for an execution.

Quincy stepped closer. "Will you please tell us what he did?"

Sean swallowed, and then he nodded. "I was only fourteen," he began slowly, "so I didn't have a driver's license or a car." He paused, swallowing. "But I had a moped," he finally said, choking. "I wish I hadn't been curious."

They waited for him to regain his composure.

He gulped, and a dull look of resignation came over his face. "It wasn't very far to Orwells, so I took a shortcut and got there just as Dad did. Once he had the backhoe loaded, he didn't drive very fast, so I was able to follow him."

"Where did he go?" Quincy asked, her voice barely a whisper.

"He drove up into the hills."

"What did he do?" It was frustrating having to drag it out of him.

"He buried a car."

"Will you show us where he buried it?" Delton asked.

Sean nodded, his whole being miserable.

"Let's go right now. You ride with us."

~

Delton almost thanked Quincy when, as if reading his thoughts, she climbed into the back seat and left the front passenger one for Sean. She scooted to the middle of the back and positioned herself between him and Sean where she had a clear view of the road ahead. There was minimal conversation as he followed Sean's instructions and drove to the house where her parents had lived.

Sean directed them to a narrow dirt lane down the road past the house. The hills rose sharply behind the property, a rugged haven for wildlife.

Delton turned on it, bounced over the ruts, and began winding uphill beneath a canopy of tree branches. As they traveled slowly upward through the woods, he observed peripherally how drawn and ashen Quincy's face was as she scanned the terrain each side of them. He fought the shiver that threaded down his back.

As the terrain rose, he heard her breathing become labored behind them. The quiet, shrouded forest had to feel ominous to her.

Sean peered to their left and right in succession. "This is the road, but I've never been back up here since then," he said uneasily. "I don't remember how far up it was. And it looks different, more overgrown and …spooky."

So he wasn't the only one feeling the shivers. Delton knew Quincy had to be affected even more deeply. He wished he could comfort her, hold her. But he had to stay focused. He aimed that focus on Sean. "Tell me if you see anything familiar, anything at all."

Minutes seemed eternal as Delton inched his way along the narrow forest trail, glancing repeatedly at Sean for any sign of recognition.

Suddenly the man leaned forward, studying the area ahead and to the right of them. When they drove alongside a clearing, he ordered, "Stop. I think the shape of this open space looks right, and it's about the distance I remember riding up here."

Delton braked to a halt, and all three of them lunged out of the truck. He went to Quincy's side, noting the drawn look in her face as they walked beneath the whispering trees. Thick undergrowth crunched beneath their feet as they kept pace with Sean.

Sean stopped and stared around him for several moments. Then he edged to his right, peering at the ground. He stopped again and began pushing leafy debris aside with his right foot. As he did, a slight indentation became visible in the ground. When he continued clearing the dirt along a line, Delton whispered, "Stay here," to Quincy and began shoving debris with his feet, estimating the angle from Sean's cleared line until they had cleared a rectangular area.

He stepped over next to Sean. "This is it, isn't it?"

Sean nodded, heavy sorrow etched in his expression. He started to speak, but couldn't.

"Why don't you go sit in the truck while I call my department and then speak to Quincy. Thank you," he added as Sean nodded, turned, and headed to the truck, his shoulders hunched.

Delton hoped having found this, whatever it was, would

bring the tortured man some closure at not having to carry the secret around with him anymore. *Please help him, Lord,* he prayed silently. Reaching out to God brought a measure of comfort to himself.

He called Chief Crenshaw and reported what they had found. Then, after being assured that officers and a metal detector would be there as soon as possible, he returned to where Quincy stood still as a statue. "Let's sit in the truck and wait for the help that's coming."

She walked robot-like beside him and offered no objection when he assisted her into the back seat and climbed in beside her. It gave Sean some privacy—and allowed Delton to be near Quincy. It wasn't wise, but that didn't seem to matter.

Fifteen minutes later, officers arrived. Quincy and Sean both watched in horrified fascination as Captain Martin began sweeping the area with the detector. Delton hated to leave them, but needed to speak to the man. He exited the pickup and approached the captain. "Is it down there?"

Martin looked up. "Something sure is. It's big, and it's metal. Do you want to take those two," he nodded toward the truck, "home while we tape off the scene and get the crime lab truck out here? I understand your regular boss is getting antsy to have you back in Springfield."

Delton winced. "I'll call him and explain that this case is at a point I can't leave it. How's Ron's leg?"

"He's getting around well enough that he says he thinks he can be back on active duty in another week or so. He asked me to thank you for helping out in his absence. Doesn't Miss Clark live in Springfield?"

"She does, but I'm sure she plans to stay here until she gets the answers she came to find."

Martin gave him a knowing grin. "Go take care of her."

Delton returned to the truck and opened the driver's door. "I can take you both home now."

"Thanks." Sean was visibly relieved.

Quincy shook her head. "I'd go crazy sitting there wondering. I want to stay and watch this."

"It'll take hours, and I'm sure they won't finish today. How about I take you home, and then bring you back in the morning?"

She didn't answer for several long moments, her gaze locked on the scene in front of them. Then she drew a long breath of capitulation. "Okay."

Chapter 19

Tuesday was a long day following a sleepless night, yet Quincy was too wired to feel sleepy. Delton picked her up at eight and drove back to the hillside excavation site, where he parked a distance away and explained that she would not be allowed any closer. But he opened the glove compartment door to reveal a pair of binoculars before he left.

She sat rigid, watching the backhoe remove dirt until her neck ached. By mid-morning a van from the local TV station had arrived, signifying that word had gotten around about the find. She took her phone from her pocket and dialed Gary while watching the busy scene.

"I'm coming down there to see you so you can give me the complete story, or as much as you can," he declared as soon as she explained. They chatted briefly and disconnected.

Quincy spotted Delton in a small cluster of men, but the main action was the skillfully maneuvering backhoe. To one side, the police captain was speaking to a TV news crew.

At noon, Quincy was surprised when Logan Fuller walked up beside the pickup and handed a fast food bag through the open window. "I called Delton and told him I'd bring lunch for the three of us."

As she accepted it, Delton appeared behind him. "Thanks, Buddy. I owe you."

"You're the one helping us out down here," Logan brushed off the thanks. "The least we can do is feed you. How's it going?"

Delton shrugged. "It's slow but steady. If things go well, they think they'll have the car excavated by the end of the day." When he went around and slid behind the wheel, Logan scooted into the back seat. The three of them downed sub sandwiches and sodas quickly.

"Do you want to go back to Holly's?" Delton asked after Logan had left.

Quincy shook her head. "I have to stay. Dad's coming this evening. He's independent, but he can't navigate his wheelchair in this terrain. He wants the story, though."

Delton nodded. "I knew that's what you would say, but I thought I would ask anyhow."

"Have you found anything yet?"

He winced. "Not yet. And I need to get back over there."

Quincy watched him return to the work scene. When he disappeared from sight behind the backhoe, she leaned back and lolled her head against the seat, unable to prevent the visions of that car—and what might be inside it. A tear trickled down her cheek.

The day stretched interminably, but late in the afternoon Delton returned to the pickup and slid inside. Lines of weariness etched his face. And more.

She came erect in the passenger seat. "Have you learned anything you can tell me?"

He turned in the seat and took her hand in his own. "We found a license plate. In spite of being underground for so long, we were able to make out the number and did a plate run. The tags to that car were registered to Drake and Janet Clayton."

She gasped at the confirmation, but quickly regained her

composure. The moment of truth was near, and she had to be strong. She bowed her head and closed her eyes. Only after a brief conversation with God, followed by Delton's departure, did she return to her vigil.

An hour later, her phone rang.

"I'm at the edge of Branson," Gary said when she answered. "Where will you go that I can meet you when you leave the crime scene?"

She told him how to find Holly's house. "I don't know what time I'll be there. Delton told me they found a license plate and verified that the car belonged to the Claytons. I don't think that's been released to the media yet."

"Thanks for the heads up. Maybe he'll have more news when you get out of there."

Weary from sitting, Quincy took the binoculars from the glove compartment, exited the pickup, and took up a stance in front of the hood. The fresh air felt good, even though it was hot. Spectators had parked along each side of the narrow road, and deputies were ordering them to leave. The excavation crew and officers were digging with shovels at different points along the periphery of the rectangular excavation site.

She stood there, transfixed, as personnel attached a cable to the car, and then it was hoisted from the grave with heavy equipment that had arrived earlier. The sight of it was sad. It was so rusty and deteriorated that she could only imagine what it was like inside. Musty, unpleasant odors drifted across the field to her.

When she saw someone clear a portion of a side window and peer inside, Quincy's stomach rolled. The man motioned, and another person began taking pictures.

Then, while the car was being loaded onto a tow truck, Delton emerged from the cluster of workers and walked toward Quincy. As he approached, she read his somber expression.

"It's them, isn't it?"

Rather than giving an immediate answer, he removed the binoculars from her hands, placed them on the hood of the truck and pulled her to him. "We found a wallet and purse with their IDs in them."

She stared over his shoulder. "I knew it had to be. It hurts. But at least I now know they didn't abandon me."

He pulled back and looked into her face. "I have one more piece of information."

Her breath hitched. "What?"

"There's a bundle in the back seat. The cloth wrapping is decayed and discolored, but it looks like a baby blanket, and the fragments inside it are identifiable. It's a doll."

Quincy stared up into his eyes, her body numb. Then she began to tremble.

"Whoever did this thought it was me back there," she whispered.

"That's what I think." He pulled her back against him, pressing her head against his chest. "You're going to be okay."

She pulled away and wiped at her eyes. "All these years someone thought I was buried here with them. What a shock it must have been to learn of my presence—and my search for them."

He nodded. "You said Gary is here. While I update the chief and order arrest warrants for Allen Ramsey and Sharleen Bledsoe, you call and tell him we'll be on our way to meet him at Holly's as soon I'm finished."

~

Delton relaxed as he realized that Gary was more concerned with the effect of their find on Quincy than scoring a story scoop for himself.

"Are you two ready to come back to Springfield?" Gary asked after a great meal at Holly's. He, Delton, and Holly's husband were having coffee in the living room while Holly and Quincy cleaned up from the meal after having run them out of the kitchen.

"I spoke to my police chief up there earlier today and told him I need another week down here. His department is short-handed now, but he agrees that this case is important to us as well as Branson. Our department is where Mrs. Rathburn originally reported her sister missing."

Gary nodded. "I agree. Whoever killed Quincy's parents has to be caught—if he's still around after so many years. Do you think she's safe now?"

He had to be honest. "I'd like to think so, but no one's in custody yet, and anyone who is violent enough to have killed her parents is violent enough to want to be sure she doesn't keep pressing the case."

Gary frowned. "Well, I know how much she wants justice for her parents. I'm glad you're here for her. You still are, aren't you?"

Delton understood that the man was asking about more than his daughter's physical wellbeing. "I'll do everything I can to protect her," he promised.

"Thank you. And thanks for the amount of story material you were able to give me. My editor is waiting for me to get it to him, so I need to go home and do the job." He set his mug on the coaster beside him and rolled his chair to the kitchen door. "I'm leaving, Quincy."

She came hurrying out to him, wiping her hands on a dish towel.

Delton stood and faced his host. "Thanks for everything." They shook hands.

He followed Quincy and Gary to the van and watched their good-byes. "I need to go," he said, stepping over near her as Gary drove away.

She turned to face him in the dusky evening light. "I've been thinking. Sean Ramsey knew more than he admitted at first. Do you think Trixie Albertson did as well?"

The sound of her voice sent little tremors of longing zinging through his nerve endings. When he reached over and drew his fingertips along the side of her jaw, she didn't pull away.

The sound of a door opening behind them broke the tenuous thread between them. "I've been thinking along the same line," he said, gathering his disorganized thoughts. "And I have a hunch. I plan to visit Trixie in the morning. I assume you want to go along?"

"Of course," she said without hesitation.

"Be ready at eight."

~

"Have you heard the news about the Claytons?" Delton asked Trixie, facing her across the employee break room table Wednesday morning. Quincy sat next to him, tension vibrating from her. They had not found Trixie at home this morning, but she had been here at the theater where she worked in the gift shop. Her supervisor had suggested she go ahead and take her break when they arrived and asked to speak with her.

Trixie shook her head, her eyes shiny on Quincy. "I did. And I'm so sorry." Her voice cracked.

"You thought a lot of them?"

She nodded jerkily. "I loved them."

Quincy looked like she wanted to hug the woman.

"Did you spend much time around them?"

A hand went over Trixie's mouth, her face crumpling in pain. "I often saw them at the theater when I was there after school waiting for my mom to get off work."

"Did you ever work in the theater?" He needed to get her to relax. It was easy to see that hearing of their deaths had upset her.

She nodded. "During the summer when I wasn't in school, they sometimes let me help Mom with her cleaning. But that was just during that last summer."

"You were what, fifteen then?"

She nodded.

"Do you know how we found them?"

She looked up, her expression puzzled. "I only heard

that you found them, and their car buried. I don't remember hearing why you looked for them in that particular place."

That information had been held back to protect Sean—and in hopes of finding out if anyone else knew that detail. Trixie seemed unknowledgeable. "How did you feel about the other couple who owned the theater?"

She shrugged. "The Ramseys were nice enough, and I really liked Sean. Sometimes his dad would give him money and tell him to get sodas or snacks for us."

"What about his mother?"

"She was okay. She wasn't around the theater as much before and after the shows. I think she and Mrs. Clayton looked after their homes, and the men took care of business matters at the theater."

"We talked to their son Sean again, and he admitted seeing his dad bury that car. He showed us where to look."

Her eyes rounded in horror as a hand moved to her mouth. "That's why …"

"What?" he asked when she came to a halt.

Her head shook slowly in denial. "He changed," she finally said. "He seemed sad, didn't laugh as much. He stopped hanging out with me."

"Let's back up a little. You said you sometimes worked at the theater with your mom. Did you ever do any other work, maybe of a personal nature, for either of the couples? The Claytons had a little girl, so they must have needed a babysitter on occasion."

Trixie's gaze darted to Quincy. She swallowed.

"Did you ever babysit for them?"

At that she crumpled forward, her head on her folded arms on the table, and sobbed brokenly. It struck Delton that two young people had been deeply affected by whatever had happened. He waited for her to become calmer. Beside him, he noted tears leaking from Quincy's eyes.

When Trixie had calmed, she sat upright and wiped her face. "I did," she said, as if accepting a dire fate.

"When was the last time you saw the Claytons?"

"The day they disappeared." She sat and spoke woodenly.

"Were you babysitting?"

She nodded. And then she looked at Quincy, her mouth trembling. "I'm so sorry."

Quincy leaned forward on the table. "Why? What did you do?"

"Just tell me your story," Delton said when Trixie remained frozen. "We just need to know the truth. I suspect you saved Quincy's life."

That seemed to reduce some of the fear in her expression. She wet her lips, drew a breath, and began speaking slowly. "It was a Saturday, so I didn't have school. Weekends were mostly when I babysat. They had heavier show schedules then, and I was free. They left the baby with me that morning. My mom had to go to work later in the day," she added before pausing to catch her breath.

"So you and the baby were alone?" he asked, knowing that Trixie's mother had been a divorced single parent who worked a lot of hours at the time.

Trixie nodded. "Mom worked her own shift and then called to say she needed to stay over and work that night in the concession stand because Betty, the woman who ran it, had to go home sick. They were friends," she rushed on, the words spilling from her once the dam had broken.

"But Janet Clayton didn't show up to get Quincy that night. So I finally took her to bed with me. I heard Mom come home sometime during the night and go to her room. Then she got up the next morning and went back to the theater to work her own shift. She didn't always work Sundays, but she did that weekend."

Quincy reached over and clasped the woman's hand. "You and I were alone, and you were taking care of me," she said softly. "Thank you."

Trixie swallowed, her mouth quivering. "I tried to call

your parents, but I got no answer."

"So, what did you do?" Quincy asked.

Trixie stared across the room, as if staring into the past. Delton eased back, okay with having Quincy ask her questions.

"I didn't have a driver's license, but I had a learner's permit. Mom had bought a newer car and hadn't sold the old one yet, so I dressed you and drove the old car out to where you lived. And I saw a U-Haul truck there. They were loading the furniture."

A sharp intake of breath sounded from Quincy. "What did you do?"

"I didn't know what to do. I had heard rumors about some bad stuff happening at the theater, but I hadn't believed them. I was scared."

"Did you tell your mom?"

Trixie shook her head. "I meant to when she got home later that day, but didn't when she came home and said the show had been cancelled because the Claytons hadn't shown up for rehearsal. The Ramseys were fit to be tied, she said."

"But they didn't call the police?"

She shook her head again. "They told everyone that they had packed up and left the state, leaving them high and dry. And they were furious about it."

"You didn't tell anyone they didn't take the baby?"

Yet another head shake. "I was in a panic. I didn't know what to do, and I couldn't tell Mom because I didn't want her to get blamed for anything."

Delton spoke up now. "So you told her Quincy had been picked up as usual?"

"Not exactly. I guess Mom just assumed she had because she didn't see her. I had her hidden in my closet."

"You were afraid something bad had happened to my parents, weren't you?" Quincy asked. "It's okay. You were young and scared."

Trixie nodded jerkily. "Mom was worried about her job,

and I was afraid for you."

Delton clasped her other hand. "You thought that if something had happened to her parents that something could happen to Quincy."

Another jerky head motion.

"So what did you do?"

"I left Quincy in my closet Monday morning and pretended to go to school. But I walked down the street and waited until Mom left for work. Then I went back to the house and got the baby. I drove to Springfield and found a children's home. I wasn't an experienced driver yet and had trouble finding it, but I finally did."

"You wrote my name and age on the infant seat, didn't you?" Quincy asked.

Trixie sniffled. "I did. And then I left you there. I cried all the way home. I'm so sorry about everything."

Quincy smiled. "Don't be sorry for saving my life. God must have guided you, because I ended up with parents who loved me and took good care of me." She stood and rounded the table.

Delton watched the two women embrace—and thanked God for sparing Quincy, the woman he suspected he loved.

Chapter 20

"There was an accomplice when we were shot at and Dad intervened," Quincy said once they were inside the unmarked car Delton was driving. "Do you think Allen Ramsey could have dragged his son into this?"

Delton started the engine. "It seems logical, but it doesn't feel right. And, although we know Allen buried the car, we don't have proof he killed them."

"Could it have been hired killers?"

"Anything is possible, I suppose."

"I can't comprehend such violence. Were they shot there in the woods, or somewhere else and put in the car before it was hauled up there? And why would someone do such a thing?"

"We're going to the police station to dig into the files some more." He drove into the street.

When they entered his office minutes later, Delton booted his computer and pulled a stack of folders from his desk. He sat and began reading, leaving Quincy free to ponder the possibilities and browse the internet on her phone.

She glanced up, meaning to ask when he thought autopsies would be completed, and observed the intensity in his expression as he leaned over the desk, as if trying to decipher something. "Have you found something?"

He didn't respond immediately. But after several moments, he looked up and gave her a grim smile. "I may have found some*one*. I'm going back over the list of casino employees that Buddy gave me, and there's a Thomas Bledsoe on it. I wonder if there's a connection to the Benny Bledsoe who's married to Ramsey's ex."

She watched as he turned his attention back to his computer and began tapping keys. It took several minutes, but then he uttered a, "yes," and whirled to face her. "He *is* Benny Bledsoe. When I typed just the last name in the search engine, I got a lot of hits. The third link I opened is an article about a Thomas Benjamin Bledsoe."

"And he married Sharleen after she and Allen Ramsey divorced."

Delton grinned. "Right." When he turned back to the computer screen and continued to read, Quincy used her phone to look up the name. Minutes later, they both looked up simultaneously. She waited for him to speak.

"He has a stepson—one with a record."

"Do you think Bledsoe and his son could have been the shooter and driver in that car?"

Delton frowned. "If there was an affair between Sharleen and an employee, namely Bledsoe, things could have gotten ugly. But I don't see how the Claytons fit into the picture. The pieces don't quite fit."

He had hardly finished the sentence when there was a tap at the door and Captain Martin stepped inside the office. "Allen Ramsey has just been arrested and brought in for questioning."

Delton bolted from his chair and started for the door, but paused next to Quincy. "I have to interrogate the man. Wait for me in here." With that, he and the captain left.

Quincy returned to her internet browsing, but didn't find anything more enlightening. Growing restless with waiting for Delton, and having nothing to do, she stood and began to pace the floor. As she did, her thoughts drifted back to when the attacks on her had begun. As she recalled that day, a shiver ran through her. But then she closed her eyes and let the memories flow in slow motion.

She recalled preparing to enter her vehicle and seeing movement around the vehicle beside her, and then the moment when a bearded guy wearing sunglasses ran up behind her and brought a cord down across her throat. The memory was bad enough, but her pulse began to pound as fresh details continued to filter through her brain.

She squeezed her eyes tighter, and details began dredging up more details from the recesses of her memory in more clarity.

Her eyes flashed open at the sound of the door opening.

Delton entered the room, his lips compressed into a grim line. "The guy lawyered up immediately."

"That's okay." She moved over next to him. "I think I know who attacked me at the Homestead."

Before she could explain, his phone rang. He raised a finger in a signal to hold the thought. "Booker."

He listened briefly. "Thanks." He disconnected and looked into Quincy's face. "That was the coroner. He said he hasn't completed the autopsies yet, but he can tell us that both of your parents were shot, one in the head, and the other in the neck."

"So they could have been sitting in the car, their upper torsos visible, when they were shot."

"It's possible. Now finish what you were telling me."

Quincy shuddered again at the recollection. "I was remembering details of being attacked at the Homestead, and it came to me that the attacker wore wedding rings. Not a band. I'm sure it was rings, because they scraped against the side of my face as that cord came down over my neck. A band wouldn't have been that rough and scratched me that way. And when I flinched and turned my head, I glimpsed a watch on the other wrist, the right one.”

He thought for a moment. Then he grinned. “You think the attacker was left handed.”

She nodded. “It was a left handed woman, dressed as a man, wearing a fake beard and big sunglasses.” She recalled an interview with such a person.

“Sharleen,” they said in unison, Delton apparently having the same memory.

At that Quincy’s common sense fled. She stepped up to Delton, placed her hands on his shoulders, and pressed a fleeting but solid kiss on his lips. Then she whirled and fled to the door.

“Wait!”

She paused with her hand on the knob, not looking back, and feeling foolish for losing control of her emotions like that.

The kiss had not been planned. She hadn’t even realized she was going to do it. She had simply felt an overpowering urge, and an emotion she couldn’t name. That truth scared her.

And now she had to face the consequences.

Steeling herself, she turned to face Delton. “That was unprofessional of me. Is there any chance you can forget about it?”

His mouth did an odd little twist, and he walked over to her. “No way.” He traced the line of her jaw with a finger and paused at the corner of her mouth. She knew she should move away, but her feet didn’t cooperate.

“This has become more than just a case,” he said, the soft tone of his voice drowning her. “It’s become personal. And I want to explore it further. But right now we have to find Sharleen.”

The opening of the door interrupted them.

Logan stepped inside. “Oops. Shall I leave and come back?”

“No, of course not,” Quincy said, welcoming the

reprieve.

~

Delton didn't know how he felt about his friend's intervention, irritated or relieved, but he needed help. "We have to find Sharleen Bledsoe, and keep her ex in custody."

"I'll get right on it." Logan backed out of the doorway.

Delton shifted his focus back to Quincy. "I can't take a civilian with me on this. I have to take you back to Holly's. And you have to stay there until we have the woman in custody."

She nodded in understanding, even though he could tell she didn't like it.

He grabbed his phone and called Captain Martin. "We need an APB on Sharleen Bledsoe. She's armed and dangerous. Her former husband is in custody, but her current husband and his son are in the area."

He had just disconnected when Logan rushed back into the room. "I couldn't track her cell phone. She's turned it off or gotten rid of it. But her credit card shows she purchased a plane ticket to France. It was due to leave an hour ago."

Delton drew a breath of frustration mixed with relief. "I guess that means she's left the country. But it also means she's no longer after Quincy."

~

Quincy was reeling at the rapid turn of events. "I don't need to go to Holly's now. I can return to the Fullers and get my camper and van," she said, excited at the prospect.

"Take her home," the captain ordered, joining them. "She's had it rough, and I'm sure she could use some recovery time while we track the woman."

She could see Delton wavering. "He's right," she said. "I need to be in my own space to relax and think." She summoned a smile in hopes of strengthening her point.

"Okay, let's go." He placed an arm behind her back and ushered her down the hall.

Traffic hadn't reached its peak yet, so the trip across

town to Logan's home didn't take long. She drank in the sight of the house that had been a haven to her and was presently unoccupied since Logan and his wife were at work and the kids at day care. She was thankful for it, but ready to be in her own space.

Delton escorted her around the side of the house to the back yard where her camper and van were parked. "I need to pick up a couple of personal items from upstairs. I'll be back in a few minutes."

She nodded. "I need to get my phone charger from my van." She also needed privacy to gather her thoughts before going inside the camper.

She had committed the error of getting emotionally entangled with her protector during a crisis. Now she had to deal with the fact that those emotions had formed in the heat of the moment and were temporary. She needed to be alone to come to grips with that.

She unlocked the door and peered inside the van. Everything looked exactly as she had left it. She rubbed a hand over the seat, barely registering the sound of a vehicle on the street.

As she reached over to the glove compartment, the sound of the motor stopped. She dug out the phone charger and backed away. As she did, another sound reached her, that of approaching footsteps. She turned—and gasped at the sight of Sharleen, a gun in her hand, marching across the lawn toward her. Cold purpose glinted from eyes that were dark slits.

Ice ran through Quincy's veins, no doubt in her mind that the woman meant to kill her, as she had murdered, or helped murder, her parents.

Help me, Lord. Please don't let her kill me.

Her thoughts flashed to Delton, the dream of a future with him that had been taking root in her mind. She'd come here searching for her past, but found something she never expected. And now it was about to be taken from her.

"Hello, Mrs. Bledsoe," she said to the menacing woman, hardly recognizing her own flat, expressionless voice. "You've already killed two people. Killing me will only make things worse. You should have taken that flight you booked."

"I changed it for a flight leaving later, right after I take care of unfinished business, in case you're interested." Her lips twisted, and her chin lifted arrogantly. But then a gleam of curiosity entered those hard, cold eyes. "You were in the back seat of that car. How are you alive now?"

Quincy stiffened her spine. "I'll tell you if you'll answer a question for me first. Why did you do it? I have a right to know." She didn't dare look at the house to see if Delton had any idea what was happening down here.

The woman winced, but the gun in her hand remained steady. She shrugged. "I don't suppose there's any reason you shouldn't know now that you're going to die for real and end this police case. There were some business things going on at the theater."

"You mean the illegal gambling and money laundering?"

A slight jerk of her head made Quincy think Sharleen hadn't expected her to be that informed. "Yes," she snapped. "That's what I mean. The goody-goodie Claytons were part of it, but decided they wanted out."

"What about other things? Was there anything personal going on that shouldn't have been?" Peripherally sensing movement at the far side of the house, Quincy kept her gaze focused on the woman and concentrated on keeping her talking, praying that Delton was there.

Sharleen took a step nearer, her right hand joining the left one that already gripped the gun. "Your daddy was good looking and talented. So was I."

Quincy fought to maintain a semblance of calm. "So you had an affair with him."

"Sure. Why not? We had some good times. But then his

wife convinced him he couldn't leave her and his kid so we could be together like we'd planned."

"That must have made you furious."

"You bet it did. We had made plans, and he suddenly did an about face." Those twisted lips twitched as she peered into the sights of the gun.

Quincy's heart thudded wildly, her skin breaking out in a cold sweat. Then she caught a glimpse of Delton at the corner of the house. He raised a finger over his lips for silence and pointed to his left, signaling his intent to circle around to where he would be behind Sharleen.

"So what did you do?" Quincy asked, careful to not betray his presence while keeping Sharleen's attention on the conversation.

"I left the theater after they did and drove to a spot on the side of the highway where I waited for them to arrive after picking you up from whoever was babysitting you that day," she continued, almost as if wanting to tell the story of her cleverness. "When their car appeared, I followed them to the road to their house. Before they could turn on it, I drove up beside them and shot the driver."

"Which one was driving?" Quincy couldn't see Delton, but she had to keep the woman talking and not risk turning her head to look for him.

"Drake was. But he wasn't supposed to be. Janet loved that car and always drove it."

Quincy stifled a gasp. "Are you saying you meant to kill my mother to get her out of the way so my dad could be with you, and killed him by mistake?" She had thought she couldn't be shocked any further, but this was mind numbing.

"That's right," Sharleen screamed.

"So then you panicked and shot her because she was a witness to what you had done."

"And then I shot the baby who was asleep in the back seat," she shrieked, insane with rage. "And now you're alive."

"It must have been quite a shock when you heard that," Quincy said through clenched teeth.

"You have no idea. Your snooping had to be stopped."

"You shot my doll," Quincy said bluntly. "For some reason, my parents hadn't picked me up from the babysitter yet. How did you get your husband to bury them?"

Sharleen's eyes rolled, but her hands on the gun held steady. "I told him I would tell the police about everything if he didn't help me."

"You mean the illegal gambling and money laundering?"

Her head jerked a nod. "And his affair with a very important man's wife." Her finger began to tighten on the trigger.

Simultaneously, Quincy flung the phone charger she still held at Sharleen's head and dived to the ground, while Delton ran up behind the woman and launched forward, tackling her to the ground and causing the shot to go wild.

Quincy scrambled to a sitting position and watched as Delton gripped Sharleen's wrist, yanked her to her feet, and began quoting her Miranda rights. When he was finished, he handcuffed the woman and plunked her back onto the ground.

Then he strode across the lawn to Quincy and scooped her into a fierce hug. "Are you okay? I was so scared when I looked out an upstairs window and saw her aiming that gun at you."

"I'm so touched," came a snide mutter behind them.

He tapped a finger on Quincy's chin. "We need to talk later." Then he pivoted to face Sharleen.

The woman gasped when he shoved his badge in front of her face, as if just realizing all she had said to Quincy— in front of a cop. She folded her arms and gave him a bitter glare. "I'm not saying another word until I have a lawyer present."

Epilogue

Delton approached Quincy's camper with resolute purpose and a touch of anxiety the next morning. He hesitated at the door and took a deep breath. She had been exhausted by the time they finished giving statements at the police station yesterday and finally arrived at the Fuller house for the evening meal that Logan insisted Dana expected them to share. There had been no privacy for the talk he and Quincy needed to have.

He closed his eyes. *Lord, give me the words she needs to hear.*

He opened his eyes at the sound of the door opening. The sight of her stole his breath.

"Breakfast is ready," Quincy said, as if expecting him.

He flashed a crooked smile at her. "I think I owe you some breakfasts." His heart pounded at the hope of providing them regularly.

"The milk was spoiled, but I still had eggs and bacon in the fridge," she explained, widening the door opening. "So I made omelets."

He stepped inside, as if arriving home after a long journey. "It sounds good."

He took the seat she indicated and bowed his head while

she said a blessing. That in itself calmed him.

He waited until they finished eating to initiate a serious conversation. "I'll be returning to my own department next week. If you'll stick around here, we can spend some time together the rest of this week. Then I'll help you hitch up this home on wheels, follow you to your dad's, and unhitch it."

She smiled, her head tilted. "I get the feeling the department here hates to lose you."

"They have a good guy chomping at the bit to return to full-time duty."

"Okay, I can stick around," she said. Then she sobered, scanning his face. "There's something I'm curious about. Did Sharleen's second husband know what she had done?"

"He says he didn't. Quite a few facts have emerged from interrogations. Sharleen and Allen had made a deal to stay together until they could sell the theater. It's not clear just when she hooked up with Bledsoe. He had only figured out her secret shortly before we spoke to him at his house. He was furious because she had dragged his son into her mess. They had been fighting about it and were splitting. So she really was gone, just not to visit relatives."

"Was the son with Sharleen the day Dad rescued us?"

"Yes. But his role isn't certain. Sharleen says he did the shooting. He says she did, but that she paid him to drive the car. We'll have to let the lawyers determine the blame on that one as well as the shooting at the Homestead parking lot. But I can identify him as the intruder at the campground."

"What about Buddy and Arnie? Were they part of it?"

"Not the killing or burying the car. They only hauled off the furniture. But they must have known the people were dead to do that. I guess Buddy will have his revenge, if that was his motive in giving us information, because Arnie will be going to prison. He and Bledsoe have both been working for Ramsey in his new gambling operation in Fayetteville."

She summoned a weak smile. "I'm glad it's over."

He reached across the small table and clasped her hand.

"You and I both heard Sharleen admit she killed your parents. We'll have to testify. I hope that won't upset you."

She looked him in the eye. "That woman murdered my parents and tried to kill me. I'll do whatever it takes to put her away."

"Good. I'll be right there with you. I think we make a good team."

She inhaled deeply. "Thank you for all you did. It was scary, but I have answers, as painful as they are. The ones I feel sorry for are Sean and Trixie, two young people who were caught up in something no fault of theirs. It caused them to carry a burden of secret guilt that impacted their lives in a harsh way."

"I'm glad about one thing. Your search led to my meeting you."

She nodded. "I'm glad about that, too."

He swallowed. "Miles and Jon have asked me to be part of their double wedding, and they both stressed that I'm to bring you. Will you attend with me?"

She smiled. "I'd love to see your friends get married."

His heart leaped. Tightening his fingers around hers, he stood and tugged her to her feet before him. He looked directly into her face. "Quincy, I know we've only known one another a brief time, but I know beyond a shadow of a doubt that you're exactly what I needed in my life and didn't know it."

Her gaze met his without faltering. "What are you saying?"

"I'm saying I love you. When I saw that woman about to shoot you, I knew I couldn't bear it if anything happened to you."

As she continued to stare at him, he nearly panicked. "I know you haven't had time to know me very well, but I'm hoping and praying that we can spend time together so ..."

She reached up and placed a finger across his lips. "If you're going to say so I can get to know and learn to love you, there's no need."

He stared at her, not certain what she meant—but hoping.

A radiant smile spread across her face. "Delton, you were special from the moment I met you. I love you with all my heart. I hope that's what you wanted to hear."

He gulped. "You do?"

She nodded. "I do. And I'll be happy to say those words in front of my pastor if you'd be interested."

"Interested doesn't begin to describe it," he said, pulling her into his arms as his heart shouted, "Whoopee!"

Then he cradled her face between his palms, leaned over, and gave her a kiss that rocked his world—and hers, if her reciprocation was any indication.

"When?" he asked when it ended.

She tipped her head, studying him. "I have to start school in just over a month. Do you think you could work it into your schedule the beginning of August? Or is that too soon?"

His skin felt as if it would crack from the grin that crossed his face. "It can't be too soon. And I'm sure Erin and Ginger will help us pull it together."

With that, he pulled her to him again, unaware of Logan's presence at an upstairs window, smiling broadly as he focused on their image framed in the small camper window.

BOOKS by Helen Gray

ROMANCES
Ozark Sweetheart
Ozark Reunion
Ozark Wedding

Bandit Bride
Prairie Bride

Bootheel Bride
Bootheel Bachelor
Bootheel Betrothal

Show Me Love
Heartland Illusions
Mozark Vision
Missouri Catch

Schoolhouse Justice
Small Town Injustice
Workplace Danger

Paige's Proposal
Brooke's Bargain
Haley's Hero
Kelsey's Keeper

NOVELLAS
River Town Romance
(2 in 1, Hawthorn Hope &
Tree of Hope)

Love Blooms
(2 in 1, Pasque Plight &
Black-Eyed Susan's Secret)

Mother Road Matches
(2 in 1, Shamrock Ruby &
Dream Team)

Secrets in the Park

Gift Bride
(Sequel to Dodge City Duos)

A Time to Love

MYSTERIES
Educated in Murder
Preyed in Murder
Coached in Murder
Rivaled in Murder
Keyed in Murder
Tutored in Murder